"So you think you have me pegged?"

Jackson asked innocently.

"I did."

"And now?" he said in a rough whisper as he touched her. Just the tips of his fingers on her chin, bringing with it an intense heat.

Rain's awareness of him was so strong that it literally had her rooted to the spot. "I don't know," she said honestly. He was closer now, so close that all rational thought vanished.

"You don't know what?"

She couldn't answer. Rain knew nothing about this man who'd come into her life so unexpectedly, throwing her off center, making her think things she had no business thinking.

But none of that mattered. Because when he touched her, then slowly lowered his head to kiss her, nothing else in this world existed.

Nothing but the two of them and this one perfect moment.

PREDICTING RAIN?
Mary Anne Wilson

TORONTO • NEW YORK • LONDON
AMSTERDAM • PARIS • SYDNEY • HAMBURG
STOCKHOLM • ATHENS • TOKYO • MILAN • MADRID
PRAGUE • WARSAW • BUDAPEST • AUCKLAND

ISBN 0-373-75007-2

PREDICTING RAIN?

This edition published by arrangement with Harlequin Books S.A.

® and TM are trademarks of the publisher. Trademarks indicated with
® are registered in the United States Patent and Trademark Office, the
Canadian Trade Marks Office and in other countries.

Visit us at www.eHarlequin.com

Printed in U.S.A.

ABOUT THE AUTHOR

Mary Anne Wilson is a Canadian transplanted to Southern California, where she lives with her husband, three children and an assortment of animals. She knew she wanted to write romances when she found herself "rewriting" the great stories in literature, such as *A Tale of Two Cities*, to give them "happy endings." Over her long career she's published more than thirty romances, had her books on bestseller lists, been nominated for Reviewer's Choice Awards and received a Career Achievement Award in Romantic Suspense. She's looking forward to her next thirty books.

Books by Mary Anne Wilson

HARLEQUIN AMERICAN ROMANCE

*Just for Kids

Dear Reader,

The idea of opposites attracting is as old as time and never loses its appeal to the romantic at heart. That concept sparked the idea for book one in my current JUST FOR KIDS day-care center series, *Predicting Rain?* I created two people so different there didn't seem to be any way they could ever find each other. But, as in real life, things happen that you never expected, and the heart is as unpredictable as the weather.

Writing about Rain and Jack was touching and lots of fun, but making sure they found each other and lived happily ever after was the best part of all.

Thanks for all the positive feedback on my JUST FOR KIDS series. I hope you enjoy this story and the next two, *Winning Sara's Heart* (2/04) and *When Megan Smiles* (3/04), as much as I enjoyed writing them.

Mary Anne Wilson

Prologue

London

Jackson Ford knew how to negotiate business deals, take over multimillion dollar corporations and face down a board of directors who wanted his scalp. He could fix anything. He'd have facts and figures, bluff if he had to, or just walk out. But as he crouched in front of the tiny four-year-old girl with her silvery blond hair plaited in two braids, sitting in the oversize leather chair in his study, he didn't have a clue what to do to make things work between them.

He knew nothing about children and hadn't planned to learn. Now he had no choice. He tried to use his best I'm-being-reasonable voice when he spoke to Victoria and laid out the facts. "I have to go to Houston, Victoria. That's in Texas. I don't know how long I'll be gone. A week, but probably two or three weeks." Her huge blue eyes stared at him, never blinking, and she said nothing. She hadn't spoken since arriving on his doorstep a week ago. "I have important business in Houston, and I have to be there as quickly as possible. I don't have a choice."

She wouldn't understand the fact that he'd been the one at LynTech initiating an acquisition of a branch of an up-and-coming corporation, an acquisition that would make LynTech more viable and give it more strength. Or that the acquisition had been totally stopped when their bid became public and others started circling in a feeding frenzy. Playing hardball in business wasn't pretty, but part of the game. This was beyond hardball. She wouldn't understand that he felt morally bound to make it work, to salvage the deal. But she could understand that he had no choice in what he had to do. "I wouldn't go if I didn't have to. You understand that, don't you?" he asked the mute child.

"Darling, of course she does." He'd almost forgotten about Eve and from the sound of her throaty voice, she was inches from him, looking over his shoulder at Victoria. "She'll be fine. You've got everything in place, and besides, her father traveled all the time. This isn't new to her."

He frowned at her mention of Ian and almost flinched when he felt her press against his back. Eve. Lavender eyes, ebony hair feathered around her elegant face, willowy beauty, and very well versed in heavy-hitting corporate business coming from the Ryders, a family that had been front and center in international business for generations. A real "catch" as his mother had told him so often. Someone who understands what his life is all about. That was true and had been an important part of his decision to marry her. But he didn't like the way she was dealing with the child right now.

''This is all new to her,'' he murmured and stood. ''And new to me, too.''

He had a flash of his image in the windows behind where Victoria sat. A tall man, two inches over six feet, not handsome in any traditional sense, with dark-brown hair brushed back from a face that was a bit too strong and a bit too irregular. Eve stood behind him. They'd been set up by mutual friends, and the timing had been right for both of them. Eve was just through a bad relationship, and he'd been considering solidifying his personal life for a while. A month ago, they'd gotten engaged, and a week ago, he'd received the phone call about Ian and Jean.

He looked down at the child who hadn't moved or taken her eyes off of him. ''Victoria, I have to go. Do you understand?''

She sat very still, her tiny hands clutching an old rag doll in the lap of the pink pinafore Eve had bought for her. She gave no indication that she cared what he was saying. If she'd only talk, and say, ''Yes, I understand, Uncle Jack,'' but that wasn't going to happen.

When he'd agreed to be the child's godfather, when he'd agreed to take care of her if Ian and Jean couldn't, none of them had ever dreamed he'd ever have to make good on his promise. That he'd be dealing with a four-year-old who lost both her mother and father in one fell swoop, who suddenly found herself in the care of a thirty-seven-year old man who worked twenty hours a day, and who'd thought that marriage wouldn't be a major change in his life. But this child *was* a major change.

''Victoria, I—'' His words were cut short as she

suddenly scooted off of the chair, and hurried past both him and Eve. He turned and saw her cross to the nanny in the doorway.

Mrs. Ferris, a slender, gray-haired woman in a deep-lavender dress and sensible oxfords, watched as the child stopped in front of her. The nanny patted the child on the head as she looked past her at Jack.

"Sir," she said in her soft Scottish brogue. "It is bedtime for the wee one. Can she come with me now?"

He hated that degree of relief he felt that Victoria was leaving the room. "Of course. Good night, Victoria."

The child didn't acknowledge what he'd said, just went with the woman without a backward glance. "What a mess," Jack muttered, closing his eyes as he ran a hand over his face.

Eve was there, her hands covering his, their fingers entwining as she drew his hands down between them. He met her sultry gaze, more than a little aware of the way her all white, short dress showed off her cleavage and her tanned legs that seemed to go on forever. "Darling, don't worry so," she said softly. "Everything's under control." She came closer, pressing her hips against his. "Everything."

He felt her against him, and wondered why he didn't feel anything except frustration over the lack of control he seemed to be having in his life. "I wish that were true," he said.

She frowned. "I know it's sad that Ian and Jean are gone, and that Victoria is an orphan."

"He was my best friend. We knew each other since college." They'd been as close as brothers back then, two men from totally different backgrounds, but who had formed a friendship that had lasted over the years. Six months ago, Ian and Jean had come to London. Now they were gone. "I never dreamed this would happen."

"I know, I know," Eve said softly. "It's hard." She frowned slightly. "And the wedding plans are piling up, decisions to be made and you're off to the States for God knows how long." Her frown deepened. "Then to suddenly have a child dumped on you." She shrugged with a degree of distaste. "It's really quite an inconvenience."

Her choice of words startled him. *Dumped?* An *inconvenience?* He'd been raised by nannies, but he'd had his parents there in the background, no matter what kind of parents they'd been. "I don't think that Ian and Jean's dying can be called a simple inconvenience," he said tightly.

"Oh, love, of course not. I was just..." She shrugged again. "It's a terrible tragedy, but life goes on. And look what the child has now. You agreed to take over her care, and you're as rich as..." She shrugged. "Well, you're well fixed, and you'll take care of her. She has a superb nanny. Kyle and Betsy loved the woman taking care of the twins." She smiled, and the expression seemed jarring to Jack. "And she's going to have beautiful clothes. It's like dressing a little doll."

Eve had been good about this, but maybe not exactly realistic. "Everything a girl needs," he muttered with more than a touch of sarcasm.

"Exactly." She didn't catch his mood at all. "And don't worry about the child. Children are resilient and she'll adjust. Now, we just have to get you back from the States and get on with things. Go to Houston, and work your magic, then come back and we can go on vacation before the real planning for the wedding gets underway." She smiled a bit more deeply as she seemed to warm up to that idea. "Somewhere warm and sunny."

"Sure," he said, and couldn't even think about a vacation at the moment. He moved away from Eve, breaking the contact to cross to the massive desk in the wood and leather study, and reach for his briefcase. "Right now I need to get out of here. I don't want to get tied up at the airport." He sorted through the papers he had to read on the flight to Houston, dropped them into the case and snapped it shut. "I'll call you from Houston when I get in."

"Okay, you go and fix things, then get back here."

"That's the plan," he murmured as he turned to her.

She gave him a soft, lingering kiss, then drew back. "Just remember...vacation." She turned and headed for the door. "Now, I'm off to see Lady Branson to find out who designed her daughter's absolutely delicious bridesmaids' outfits last year." She stopped at the door and smiled at him. "Remember, vacation." And she left.

He heard the entry door click shut behind Eve. Even through the thick walls of the century-old row house, he heard Eve's sports car's motor rev to life, then drive off in a squeal of tires. The next moment, Mrs. Ferris appeared in the doorway. Her expression was somber, but then again, that seemed to be her normal appearance. "The driver is at the side door with your car, sir, and the wee one is in bed, one light on, eyes closed. She did not have her milk, just refused it, and wore the pink nightie Miss Ryder bought for her. I hope that is acceptable.''

He turned and said, ''Yes, it is.''

''She has that doll with her, too. I think it might be close to a health hazard. Both the doll and its clothes need cleaning.''

That was the least of his worries. ''Buy her a new doll.''

''That is not it, sir,'' she said, with more than a touch of reproach in her voice. ''She would not want a new doll, but that doll is dirty, and I just wanted to mention it so you know that I'm aware of the dangers.''

He was quite certain Mrs. Ferris was aware of everything, and he didn't want, or need, a blow-by-blow description of what she knew or didn't know. ''Do whatever you think is best,'' he said, his tone a bit more clipped than he'd intended.

''As you wish, sir,'' she murmured.

''You have all my phone numbers, my contacts at LynTech, and my e-mail address,'' he said as he gripped the briefcase. ''If anything comes up, Miss Ryder can assist you. The bottom line is, just give the child whatever she needs.''

''That's another thing, sir.'' She crossed her arms on her chest. ''I was always believing that spoiling a child, no matter what the reasons, was wrong. Children need rules and schedules. Trust me, that gives a child a sense of security.''

She was probably right. What did he know about kids? He and Eve hadn't even talked about children, and the only real contact he'd had with children before this, had been when he was a child himself. "Of course," he murmured.

"It is just my opinion, sir."

He exhaled as he frowned at the gray-haired woman. "Mrs. Ferris, can we get one thing straight?"

Her lips tightened slightly. "Of course, sir."

"I don't know much about children, and I don't have the time to learn right now. That's what I'm paying you for, to leave me out of the loop, unless there is a major problem. I trust your professional instincts to do the right thing, so you don't have to run everything past me. Do you understand?"

Her face flushed slightly. "Yes, sir," she said.

"Good. Now, tell Victoria goodbye for me, and I'll contact you when I get to Houston."

"Yes, sir. Safe trip," she said and left quickly.

He headed out of the room, and down the narrow wood-lined hall toward the side entrance. A soft sound stopped him, and he looked up the back stairs. It was shadowy, but he saw Victoria on the top step, sitting with her doll, rocking.

"Victoria?" he said, and started up, but Mrs. Ferris was there.

"Don't trouble yourself, sir, she's okay, just a mite restless." The nanny reached down and took Victoria's hand, urging her to her feet.

"Mrs. Ferris?"

"Yes, sir," she said, the lady standing by the little girl in the semishadows.

"Stay with her until she falls asleep, and—" he exhaled "—do that every night."

"As you wish, sir," she said, and the two of them

went silently out of sight into the upper hallway. Jack took a deep breath. He had to leave. He couldn't change that. When he got back, he'd worry about the wedding plans and about a silent four-year-old girl. Right now he had to focus on Houston and what was waiting for him there.

Chapter One

Jack had barely landed in Houston when the phone rang in the company car. As the driver drove out of the airport, Jack answered the phone. "Jack? Zane. Glad you made it in."

Zane Holden, one of the two men who took over LynTech from the founder, Robert Lewis, sounded rushed and anxious. "What's going on?" Jack asked, settling back in the soft gray leather.

"We're just waiting for you before we make a move toward Sommers."

"He's in Houston?"

"Not yet. He's in New York at the moment. If we get lucky, he'll agree to handle the negotiations himself, instead of using a middleman."

E. J. Sommers, the founder and head of the EJS Corporation, wasn't an easy man to pin down. He didn't do things the way other corporate heads did. He was more freewheeling, more unstructured, and that bothered Jack. But the branch of EJS Corporation that LynTech wanted was a gem. A real find. "Any word on how our interest in EJS got out?"

"We'll talk about that when you get here. I called

Robert Lewis in on it as a consultant. We need his take on things.''

''That's a smart move. No one knows the business around here like Robert.''

Robert Lewis had been Jack's father's friend from college days, just the way Ian had been his. Ten years ago, when Jack's father had died, Robert had been there. Robert had known the full story about Jack's father, and he'd been the one to trust Jack to make things right. He owed Robert a lot and, despite the fact that the company wasn't Robert's any longer, it meant a lot to the man, and Jack wasn't going to let him down.

''Did you find a nanny?'' Zane asked.

Jack grimaced as he remembered his last glimpse of Victoria alone at the top of the stairs. He was surprised that the co-CEO of LynTech was worried about a nanny. He'd dealt with Zane for over a year, and knew that his son, Walker, was the center of his existence along with his wife Lindsey, but he didn't expect him to take much of an interest in his child care situation.

''It's all settled,'' he said and realized that he'd just uttered a lie of staggering magnitude.

''Good. The child, the little girl, is she okay with the nanny?''

That was when he realized why Zane was asking. It wasn't the child he was asking about, he was asking if Jack was in any condition to give one hundred percent to the problem at hand. That annoyed him slightly, that Zane would even think that he wouldn't be effective in a crisis. ''She's fine with the nanny, and she understands I had to leave.''

''I never found a good nanny when I needed one.''

He knew enough about Zane to know what he was referring to, when his son had been dropped into his life. When Lindsey, now his wife, had stepped in to be a mother to the boy, and they'd become a family. There was a vague similarity between his and Jack's predicaments with child care, except Victoria wasn't his, and…well, Eve was Eve. She'd stepped right in, too. She'd found Mrs. Ferris and promptly bought Victoria a whole new wardrobe. She smiled at the child, pouted about her private time with Jack being limited, then blissfully went on with her plans.

''My fiancée found the nanny through a friend,'' he said, thinking that maybe Eve didn't have overwhelming maternal instincts, but then again, he'd never had any great paternal instincts, either.

''Lindsey thought that you could have brought the child with you and she could have been cared for at the day-care center at LynTech while you worked.''

Zane had even recruited his wife to make sure Jack was focused on the crisis. Maybe his father's reputation had preceded him with Zane. He hoped not. The car slowed and Jack looked out at the downtown street where the headquarters for LynTech were located. ''Thank her for me, but Victoria's just fine in London. We're outside. I'll be up in a few minutes, then go to the hotel later on.''

''That's another thing. The hotel's not going to work out for this. It's overrun with people involved in the charity ball that's being planned by LynTech. You wouldn't have any privacy.''

''Then where am I staying?'' he asked, caring only that he could work uninterrupted.

''No hotel rooms are available on short notice, so we decided on a loft we've got set up not far from the offices. Lots of privacy, and it's wired directly to here.''

''Fine, whatever,'' Jack murmured. ''See you in a few,'' he said and hung up as the luxury car approached the entrance for the parking garage.

SEX AND SILK. It had to be a dream, because Jack was never poetic, and he knew that he'd never met the owner of the voice that was filtering around him in the blackness.

After getting only a few hours' sleep in the last two days, Jack had counted on sleeping for six hours before getting back to work. He'd been at the offices since arriving from London, took a nap in a side room off of Zane Holden's office, and this was the first time he'd made it to the loft. He'd planned to sleep hard, then get to work on his own without interruption.

He just hadn't expected to dream, because he never dreamed. At least, he never remembered any dreams. He'd set his internal clock for a few hours and slept…his usual pattern. Get hard sleep, then work hard. But now there was a dream that consisted of a single voice, low murmurs, floating around him. Soft. Seductively feminine.

''Oh, come on,'' the voice whispered. ''Come to me.''

Sexy, inviting, seducing him, even though it barely existed.

''That's it, love. Come on. Please? Come to me. Now.''

No pictures, no images, just him listening, drifting,

waiting, the sound tingling through his body, giving him pleasure.

''Good, good.'' The whisper floated softly. ''That's it. Come on, baby, that's it. Closer, closer.''

The voice was seeping into his being, making him ache for more, then it was gone. He woke suddenly, not sure what had just happened. But his heart was pounding in his chest and his body ached, a painful remnant of his reaction to the voice in his dreams. He took shallow, rapid breaths while he stared up into the shadows overhead, trying to make his body let go of the dream.

Damn dream! He shifted onto his side, wide-awake now, but froze when he saw a dull glow coming over the partial wall that divided the sleeping area from the kitchen. When he'd come in, he had turned on the overhead lights to get oriented, showered, then turned off all the lights and climbed into the king-size bed. The only things he'd left on were the fax machine and computer, waiting for incoming messages. Now a light was on in the kitchen. He heard a shuffling sound, then a faint clink.

Someone was there.

Zane? Matthew Terrell, the other CEO? Rita something-or-other who worked for both men? He looked at the clock and the glowing LED panel read 2:13 a.m. No, Zane wouldn't be here at this time. Zane wouldn't be anywhere, but with his family. Neither would Matt or anyone else from LynTech.

He listened, heard another sound, a low humming and he moved. He stood, grabbed his pants and put them on quickly, forgoing his shirt and shoes, then debated his options. Call someone, stay quiet and hope whoever was there would leave, or go out and confront the trespasser.

He considered his options, then heard another soft sound, of a drawer being opened, then closed. He made his decision. The best thing to do was to get out of the loft without being seen, but be prepared just in case. He looked around in the shadow-darkened room for anything he could use as a weapon, and the best thing he could see was a lamp by the bed that looked solid. He reached for it, took off the shade and took out the bulb, then unplugged it and wrapped the cord around the base that felt like rough stone.

He held it like a club and it felt heavy and solid. Cautiously, he approached the door that led into the main living area of the loft. He paused, trying to remember the layout of the loft. Basically one cavernous space, divided into areas by six-foot high walls that came short of touching the lofty ceilings by at least another six feet. Polished hardwood floors, rough white plastered walls, plain furnishings, just two sprawling navy couches, a television in a unit on the far wall, a few tables, some stacked boxes, no carpets that he remembered. The communications-work area took up most of the back wall, on a twelve-foot table set up under high louvered windows, and framed by towering floor-to-ceiling windows on either side.

Simple and clear. He just had to get to the door without being noticed. He cautiously looked out into the main space, and knew luck was with him. Whoever had broken in had left the front door open enough for a thin sliver of light from the corridor to cut into the room. He glanced to his left, to the glow of a light beyond the partial wall that defined the kitchen area. Carefully, he eased into the space, staying as close to the wall as he could while he slowly made his way to the right and the escape of the open door.

He'd gone only a few feet when he heard something that stopped him in his tracks. The voice. The one from his dreams. This time it was softly singing a song he vaguely remembered from somewhere in the past, maybe an old Bob Dylan song…or some folk song? A simple melody sung in a breathy whisper. Then the song stopped when the voice said softly, "So, you don't like music, huh? Bummer."

There was no response. Just the voice again, "Okay, okay, I get the idea." Followed by a low chuckle. "I'll stop."

The idea of going out the entry door was forgotten and Jack found himself moving silently toward the kitchen, the lamp base firmly gripped. The voice. He'd been right. A feminine voice. A woman, and she seemed to be talking to herself or maybe on the telephone. He didn't have a clue if there was a phone line in the kitchen. He lifted the lamp base slightly as he approached the wall, then looked into the kitchen area.

He saw the owner of the voice that had invaded his dreams, the person who invaded the loft. It didn't make sense. She was tiny, definitely alone, not more than an inch over five feet tall, maybe one hundred pounds soaking wet and she had her back to him as she leaned forward over something on the counter. She looked tiny in an oversize T-shirt fashioned in brilliant, tie-dyed colors of reds, blues and yellows. It was barely long enough to brush the tops of her bare thighs. Her hair so blond it was almost silver, fell long and straight down her back, almost to her waist, and her feet were bare. There was something at her slender ankle, jewelry of some sort.

Whatever fear he'd had at the intrusion was gone, replaced by curiosity and something else. That stirring he'd experienced in the dream was back full-force, fed by the way her long hair shifted in a silky veil when she moved, and by the seductive lines of her bare legs. He just watched. Her hands shifted to her hips, the action hiking the T-shirt higher on her thighs while her feet shifted on the cold hardwood floor.

"Okay, bud, you're on your own," she said a little louder now, but the voice didn't lose any of its sexiness.

This was ridiculous, standing here, watching, listening. He made himself move farther into the room, still gripping the lamp base, and he made himself speak up. "What's going on?" he demanded.

She jerked around, her long hair flowing like a veil, then she was facing him. If the voice had been disturbing, looking into huge brown eyes set in a delicately boned face, seeing seductively full lips softly parted in surprise and watching her rapid breathing press her high, small breasts against the soft cotton of her shirt, stunned him. His jumbled thoughts and spontaneous responses were so unlike anything he'd experienced before with any woman, that he was literally frozen to the spot. He simply stared at her.

WHEN RAIN ARMSTRONG heard that voice, she spun around. Her heart pounded against her ribs, and she couldn't take a decent lungful of air to save her life. Fear choked her and she had to blink twice before she could make out a man not more than six feet from her in the shadowed kitchen. A man who had appeared out of nowhere in a loft that was supposed to have been deserted.

All she could do was stare at him, tall and lean, standing by the entrance, half lost in the fringe shadows of the space. She could tell he was wearing nothing but dark slacks and that he totally blocked any means of escape. He had something in his right hand, something that look ominously heavy and lethal, raised as if ready to strike her.

Even though she couldn't move, her mind raced. *Get out!* she screamed in her head. *Just get out any way you can!* But she didn't know how to do that. The only weapon she had was the can opener she had been using to open the cat food, and it was hardly a weapon.

He took a single step toward her. "I asked what's going on? What are you doing in here?"

She swallowed hard. "Wh-what are you doing in here?"

"You first," he muttered as he took another step forward.

She tried to back up, but her waist hit the counter behind her. She darted a look past him, the space between him and the door rapidly expanding. Maybe she could get around him before he could react. But then again, maybe he'd just hit her with the thing in his hands. He was tall, a good foot taller then she, somewhere in his mid to late thirties, and from his near naked state, she could see he was fit. Lightly tanned skin stretched taut over hard stomach muscles, a chest with just an arrow of dark hair and disturbingly broad shoulders. His angular face was partially shadowed in the dim light, but she could see the slash of dark brows over hooded eyes, a slightly crooked nose, all framed by dark hair, short and somewhat spiked.

She saw the way his hand held the weapon, and she cursed the fact she didn't have a clue where the knives were located. She shifted slightly, ready to just make a run for it, but she never got the chance. Joey, the orange tabby cat she'd come to feed, had made his way to the top of the wall between the kitchen and living area, and right then, the huge beast launched himself at the intruder. The man must have sensed something coming, because he started to turn in the direction of the attacking cat, but he couldn't do a thing to protect himself before there was impact.

The cat hit him in the shoulder and chest, sending him off balance, and for a moment man and cat were suspended in midair flying to Rain's right. Then there was a crashing sound as the man hit the floor, mixed with a profound curse. The cat immediately launched himself off of the man, up and onto the counter in one smooth move.

It was Rain's chance to escape, and she took it, but she'd only taken one step before her foot struck something hard and cold. She pitched forward, flailing to get her balance, but fell straight into the prone stranger.

There was heat and the scent of soap and maleness, and strength. That scared her. She quickly pushed as hard as she could, sending herself back and away from the contact, hitting the wooden floor and ending up on her knees. She sat back on her heels, pushed her tangled hair out of her face. Whatever chance she had of escape was gone.

The man was standing and towering over. Then she saw the weapon he'd been holding, the thing that had caused her to trip. She made a grab for it, but she wasn't fast enough. He had it and he was standing over her once again.

She took several deep breaths, then pushed herself to her feet. She couldn't do a thing about his size advantage, but she could talk a good game—her father had always told her that, insinuating that was why she was so good at what she did. She took another breath, thankful that the man was keeping his distance, at least for now. She didn't want to touch him again or have him touch her.

She braced herself, ready to try anything, then looked right at him, but he wasn't looking at her. He was frowning at Joey on the counter. "What in the hell is that?"

"My attack cat," she muttered, her mind working a mile a minute. The best defense is a good offense, and she'd go on the offensive to see what happened. "You're lucky all he did was knock you down, you sneaking in here like this and scaring me to death."

He looked at her then and she had the oddest feeling she'd met him before. But she hadn't. She'd never heard that voice or faced the man himself before in her life. She would have remembered. "What was he going to do, tear me to shreds?"

She shrugged. "Who knows?"

He shook his head. "Just tell me why you're here

and what in the hell you're doing here at two in the morning?''

At least he was talking and not bashing her over the head with the lamp base. An attacker who wanted to talk, but why was he here half-dressed? It didn't make sense. ''You explain first,'' she said.

He exhaled roughly. ''Oh, come on. I'm not the one who broke in.''

''I didn't break in. There's a key in the lock.'' She knew at least one thing. ''That's how you got in here, isn't it? I left the damn door open.''

''No, I have my own key,'' he said.

Her stomach sank. ''You were in here all along?''

''Since midnight.''

Oh, boy, had she been wrong. ''In here?''

''Actually, in the bedroom. I was sleeping....'' He shrugged. ''Let's start over. It's obvious that you aren't here ripping me off, and I belong here, so just tell me why you're here in the middle of the night with that animal?''

He was staying here. She knew people went in and out of this place, but no one had told her that anyone would be here tonight, or she wouldn't have come over. She motioned to Joey who was calmly cleaning himself on the counter. ''Feeding that beast.''

''At two in the morning?''

''That wasn't my idea,'' she muttered and looked at the lamp base in his hand. ''Were you going to hit me with that?''

He looked taken aback, but said, ''Only if you were a killer and you outweighed me by fifty pounds.''

''Well, I'm not and I don't,'' she muttered.

''So I can see,'' he said softly in a tone that brought

color to her cheeks. Then he said, "So, you came to feed the cat…?"

She exhaled and motioned to the lamp base. "Can you put that down?"

He eyed her up and down, and there was a definite softening in his expression. She realized that his eyes weren't just shadowed, they were dark as night. "If you promise not to unleash that beast on me again."

"Sorry, I can't promise that. He's pretty much got a mind of his own."

"Okay, but I'll keep an eye on him," he said and laid the lamp base on the counter. Facing her again, he asked, "Now, why were you coming in here to feed him at this time of night?"

"Because he ran away."

"From you?"

"No, the guy who used to live here. He moved, the cat went with him, but he disappeared—the cat, not the man—and his wife's worried about it and thought that the cat might try to get back here, and sure enough…" She pointed to Joey. "He turned up tonight. I was sitting on the fire escape meditating when I spotted him going over the roof, then he jumped down to the window and disappeared. I guess the guy left the window open just in case he came back. Anyway, he got in, and I knew…" She cleared her throat. "I thought this place was empty."

"Wrong," he said. "So, you were outside on the fire escape, then came in here? What do you do, hang out on fire escapes at night for fun?"

She shook her head. "I'm staying in the next unit. The guy, the one who lived here and moved out with the cat—"

"I've got that part of it."

"Okay, well he asked if the cat showed up, could we feed him or something and keep him here until he could get over here to take him back. So, I did. Not that he liked the food I found." She took a breath. "I thought he was waiting here in an empty loft, and I came over." She shrugged. "And there you were."

He raked his fingers through his hair, spiking it even more. "Who was it who asked you to watch for the cat?"

"Zane something-or-other, one of the suits at LynTech, I think. They lease this place, for whatever reasons. Since I've been here, no one's lived in here at all for more than a few days."

"One of the what at LynTech?"

"Excuse me?"

"You said one of the suits at LynTech? A suit?"

"A suit. You know, some bigwig executive who makes millions and wants to rule the world from his corporate tower. Although this isn't any corporate tower, and I'd think, with all the money they're raking in, that they could put their people up in a plush penthouse or something."

His expression tightened. "Zane Holden wants to the rule the world?"

"Whatever. The man's the head of everything at LynTech, along with some other guy, and, from what I've heard, eats up competitors. Heck, he's probably eyeing IBM even as we speak."

"You've met him?"

"Oh, of course not. And I can't say I'd want to."

"Not your type, huh?"

She heard the edge to his voice, then suddenly it

all added up. She was so slow on the uptake, it had to be the late hour and inability to sleep that was fogging her brain. He was here, in a place leased by LynTech. He more than likely worked for Holden. He was a suit. A half-naked suit at the moment, but a suit, unless he was just loft sitting or something. Maybe a relative in from out of town? "I wouldn't know," she murmured.

He eyed her night shirt and bare feet. "Take my word for it, he's not your type."

She felt that touch of heat in her cheeks again at the tone in his voice. Condescension, or maybe sarcasm? She wasn't sure, but she knew that she didn't like it. "Tell your boss his cat is back," she said.

"My boss?" he asked.

The moment he said the words, she knew she'd been wrong. This man wasn't a flunky. He was a boss, a filthy rich boss staying in a very plain loft. She remembered exactly where she'd seen him before. A glossy magazine. She'd been in one of the offices at the hospital waiting for yet another interview with Dr. Shay, and she'd picked it up to pass the time. It had been one of those "people on the go" columns, the type that either started rumors or confirmed them.

This man had earned a full half-page column including a color picture. He'd been in a tux, his arm around the shoulders of a tall, beautiful woman with perfect bone structure and a cap of ebony hair. The paragraph was about Jackson Ford, and Eve something-or-other. Definitely a suit, a very rich, powerful suit. It had been announcing the engagement of Jackson Ford, head of European operations for LynTech. Something about them making their home in London.

''You're Jackson Ford, aren't you?'' she blurted out. She'd definitely shocked him.

''How in the hell—?''

''Saw your picture in a magazine a bit back. You were getting engaged and partying in England, I think.''

''You got me,'' he said. ''So, you are…?''

Out of here, she thought, but said, ''I didn't know you were here, that anyone was here. Sorry about all of this.''

''I didn't expect to wake up at two in the morning and find a half dressed hippie in the kitchen.''

''Hippie?''

He flicked his gaze over her. ''Hippie.''

''Whatever,'' she said, and knew it was time to get out of the loft and away from this guy. She'd faced snobbery before, but it hadn't rankled her as much as the snobbery he was showing at that moment.

''Now that we've labeled each other, I'm leaving,'' she said, and moved to go past him.

But it wasn't going to be that easy, not when he caught her by the upper arm and stopped her. His fingers hovered this side of real pain, but held her firmly, stopping her escape completely. ''Hold on there,'' he said. ''You aren't leaving yet.''

Chapter Two

Rain fought every instinct to try to free herself of his hold, and stood very still. "What, do you want me to thank you for not braining me with that lamp? Or do you want me to do a spirit dance around you while you try to correct your very-out-of-whack Karma?"

He almost smiled, and she had a flashing knowledge that he was a man who didn't smile easily. "Neither," he said and let her go. "I just wanted to know who you are."

She stayed where she was, not moving at all and definitely not rubbing her arm where he'd gripped her. "I'm an idiot who thought I was rescuing a cat. I even gave him some dolphin free tuna to eat, and he turned his nose up at it. Then you came after me with that lamp."

"I never threatened you with the lamp or anything else, and as far as my karma goes, it's just fine."

"Rainbow!"

She heard George calling from somewhere beyond the entry door and his voice cut through the loft with a boom even from that distance. "I'm in here,

George!'' she called back, not taking her eyes off the man in front of her. ''I'll be right there.''

''Okay,'' he called back and she heard their loft door close with a soft clang.

''Rainbow?'' Jack asked, the way so many people had said her given name over the years.

''Rain is fine,'' she muttered. ''George just likes to use the full version.''

''George?''

''Your neighbor. The guy Zane gave the key to in case Joey showed up?''

''Joey?''

''The cat.''

''You were talking to the cat earlier?'' he asked.

''Sure. I was trying to coax him off the wall to start with, then tried to get him to eat very expensive tuna.''

Jack kept watching her, a tiny woman who talked fast, moved with real ease and whom he'd felt against him on the floor. He took a breath, but wished he hadn't. She carried the scent of…something…sweet and soft…but elusive. And she lived next door. And all he knew about anyone else on this floor was what Zane had said.

''There's a middle-aged hippie next door to the loft, George Armstrong. He's a good man, but he's beyond eccentric and if you let him, he'll give you hours of lectures about corporate greed. He paints, I think, and comes and goes on whims, apparently. He never got past the 'do your own thing' or 'if it feels good, do it,' era,'' she said.

''You said you live next door?''

''I moved in a few weeks ago. George is my—''

''I know all about George,'' he said before she

could go into their relationship. He understood all too well from what Zane had told him. But it bothered him that she was involved with the man.

She frowned, then cocked her head to one side and her hair moved in a soft veil. "Oh, sure, of course, you know."

"What does that mean?"

"Just more labeling. Since George doesn't conform to what you think he should, you're sure that he's some irresponsible hippie living like some flower child." She bit her lip. "Gad, you're a snob."

A snob? "Now I'm a stuffed suit and a snob?"

She shook her head, then went past him into the main living area that was deep in shadows except for the light slicing in from the hallway. He followed her, watching her silhouetted against the light coming in the door. She was at the entrance before she stopped and turned back to him. In that fleeting moment, the light behind her softly exposed her slender figure. "Sorry for the intrusion. I'll let that Zane person know the cat's back."

"Don't bother. I'll take care of it," he said.

"Oh, sure, the responsible one," she muttered.

She was going back to that middle-aged hippie and he felt vaguely sick. "I'll take care of it," he repeated.

"Of course, and, oh, by the way, my name's Rainbow Swan, for the record. Good night, Jackson Ford."

With that, she left, quietly closing the door behind her. Before he could do more than absorb the fact that she'd obviously had the last word, the door opened again and this time he could see through the thin cotton of her T-shirt. "I've got the key," she said. "Tell Zane that he can come get it any time he wants to. But until then we'll guard it with our lives so that you'll be safe from any and all undesirables who might be in the area." And she closed the door after her.

Jack crossed to the door, opened it and heard another door shut firmly. Rain was gone. And she'd had a double last word. He hated that. He closed his door, threw the bolt lock on it, then saw the cat. The animal was walking silently along the shelf on the top of the partial wall. He got to the bedroom area, looked at Jack, then leaped in the opposite direction and disappeared. A cat. A hippie. He looked at the clock. The whole thing had lasted fifteen minutes, tops. It had seemed to last forever.

The middle-aged hippie and Rain. It sounded like the title of a bad novel, or some crazy song. But it knotted his stomach with distaste. Instead of going to the bedroom, he crossed to the work station, turned on two lights and sat down in front of the computer. As the monitor warmed up, he heard the cat somewhere close by mewing softly in the darkness. Then a heavy thump came from somewhere beyond the wall across the room that was shared with the next loft.

He looked at the computer screen, logged onto the Internet and went to the mail program. There were several notes from Mrs. Ferris, and a single note from Eve. He opened Eve's note quickly. All thoughts of Rain pushed to the back of his mind…for now.

RAIN WENT INTO the loft and called out to George. "I'm back." She crossed to the kitchen to make herself a cup of green tea.

"What was going on over there?" he asked coming up behind her.

"Labeling," she muttered, a bit shocked that Jack Ford had gotten under her skin so completely. Labels didn't matter. She'd known that all her life, but for some reason his attitude stung.

"What?" George asked as Rain put the teakettle on the stove, then turned to her father.

Yes, he was a hippie. From the long gray hair, thin on top, pulled back in a ponytail with a friendship rope that Bree, her mother, had made for him, to the rope sandals, the six earrings in his left ear and the cutoffs worn with a shirt that sported a skull and roses on it, he was a hippie. Although Rain liked the term *a free, caring spirit* better than *hippie*. He was middle-aged, sincere about helping to make the world a better place, and vastly talented as a painter.

She glanced at the loft, a cavernous space free of any real adornments, with pillows instead of chairs, bed pads on the floor in the side alcoves, and his paintings all around, in various stages of completion. "Want some green tea?" she asked, not about to get into this with her father, too.

He waved that aside with, "No, thanks," and headed over to his latest canvas, a huge, four-by-six-foot work in progress that he'd labeled Experimental. *Red* he called it, and it was that. Very red. Lines, sweeping swirls, dots, splashes, all in various shades of red. Even though she loved her father and thought he was beyond talented, it still amused her at George's chagrin that "normies," as her dad called the rest of the world, actually liked his work and bought it. "The cat showed up, huh?"

"Sure did," she said and turned as the kettle started to whistle. As she made a mug of tea, George put on one of his tapes of lute music. She turned with the steaming mug in her hands and inhaled the combination of paint and incense in the air. "You said LynTech used that loft sometimes when their people came to town?"

"Yeah," George said, studying his painting, hands on his hips and his head cocked to one side. "They've got it set up so they can work without ever seeing the light of day," he said. "I hear they'll need it with all that stuff going on at LynTech."

"What stuff?" she asked.

"Something big, and I don't mean that charity ball next month." He looked away from his canvas and back at her. "Business intrigue that no one's talking about."

She crossed to the rope hammock by the fire escape window on the back wall and settled into it, cradling her tea. This was the way it had been whenever she was here with George, her sipping tea in the hammock, him with his painting. It felt good, even if she was twenty-eight years old. "What's the big secret?"

"I don't know, but they called in a big gun from London, Jackson Ford. He's dead in the middle of it."

"He's also dead in the middle of the loft next door," she muttered and took another sip of the tea.

George looked surprised. "You sure?"

"I just ran into him when I was feeding that cat." Now she understood a slight hint of a certain prop-

erness in his voice. England. Yes, it could be a hint
of an English accent he might have absorbed living
there. Then again, maybe it just came from him being
so incredibly uptight. "They must use that place a
lot. It's set up like a control center for NASA, every
business machine you could want. Well, not you."

"Mmm," George said as he looked back at the
painting. "Next door, huh? Well, from what little I've
been able to find out, Ford and some others are working on a big deal, and it looks as if that very big deal
could fall through."

Rain wondered if Mr. Jackson Ford was on the
edge of being booted from LynTech for some mess
up on his part? Maybe that was partly why he was so
uptight. "Too bad," she said.

"It's all a part of the corporate mindset, that need
to work your butt off and make big bucks and destroy
this country in the process," George said. "That can't
be easy on anyone."

She didn't want him to get started on this. She'd
heard the speech far too often, and her nerves couldn't
stand it now. "No it can't," she said, ready to deflect
the topic, but he did it for her.

"Do you think this is too much?" he asked, point-
ing at a huge blot of crimson dead in the middle of
the canvas. "Too…intense, too flamboyant?"

Everything about George was flamboyant, another
character trait that she'd adjusted to a long time ago.
"You're asking me that, the person who you once
said, if I remember correctly, had the artistic bent of
a log?" she teased.

He turned with a grin. "I forgot for a moment.
Thought I was talking to Serenity."

She called her mother Bree, but George never called her by anything except the nickname he'd given her the summer they met years ago at a commune on the coast of California near Big Sur. "So, she called, didn't she?"

"Sure did." The grin seemed permanent now. He always seemed to glow a bit when he talked about her. Over the years, through all the changes in both of them, she'd never doubted that her parents loved each other very much. They just didn't commit to a relationship the way the world thought they should. "Did I tell you I'm taking off soon?" George asked.

"No, you didn't, but then again, when did you ever check in when you wanted to take off?" She'd just gotten here, and with the mess at the hospital, she was hoping he'd be around for a while. But George moved when he wanted to and she was used to him just up and leaving when the spirit moved him.

"True, and that being the case, I'm assuming that I didn't tell you where I'm going?"

"I didn't expect you would," she said. "Is there a gathering or something?"

"No, not at this time of the year." Then he came over to the hammock and stood in front of Rain with his arms out at his sides. "So, how do I look?"

She shrugged. "Like you usually look."

For some reason that seemed to please him. "Good, good," he murmured and moved across the studio area to the makeshift dining table all but covered with stretched canvases and paint supplies.

"So, where are you going?" she asked.

"The Golden City," he said, the smile deepening.

That meant San Francisco, more specifically, Palo Alto. "Oh, is she expecting you?"

"She's always expecting me," he said. "And while I'm gone, chill and get centered."

"I'm chilling, and I'm centered," she said.

"No, you're not. I can't remember how long it's been since you've been centered. That so-called institution of higher learning might have given you a degree, but it also made you uptight." He frowned at her. "And since you showed up on my doorstep saying you were going to play doctor in Houston, well…" He gave a mock shudder. "Girl, you need to get back to the basics."

She wasn't in any mood for one of his lectures on her choices. For a person who believed in free will and live and let live, he got remarkably judgmental about her life choices. For a moment she thought that despite his attempts at being so different from the suits, he and Jack Ford had something in common. Judging her. "George, stop. You know this is a nontopic. You taught me to make my own choices, and my own choice was to become a clinical therapist for children."

"I know, I know, and you're really trying to help children, just going down a different road." He came across to her. "It's just hard for me to think of you, my daughter, being a real professional with a real Ph.D." He looked genuinely shocked by that. "Who would have thought it?"

"Yeah, who would have thought it?" she murmured with a grin.

He kissed her on the forehead, then stood back and said, "I'm leaving later this morning."

She had always been amazed at her parents' idea of "marriage." Her mother lived in Palo Alto and George, whom her mother called "Dune," lived wherever he wanted to, but mostly here in Houston where he painted. But twice a year, George headed west and twice a year, Bree headed east. That had been going on since Rain was eight and her mother had decided that she needed a "home" that stayed put. So the two of them had agreed on an arrangement, and it worked. Amazingly, twenty years later, they were still "connected," and happier than a whole lot of couples held together by a piece of paper.

"Give her my love?" she murmured.

"Why don't you come out with me? She'd love to see you."

"I saw her two weeks ago when I left there to come here," she pointed out. "And you know I can't anyway, not with this whole thing at the hospital up in the air." She shrugged. "I never expected to get here, thinking the staff position at the hospital was a done deal, then to be told that there were 'budget considerations,' and they put me on hold. I talked to Dr. Shay earlier today and he said it could be a week or two before they get the approval." She shrugged. "I think they look at it as another clinical psychologist in pediatrics isn't a life and death role, not like a surgeon or an internist."

"Don't they know that the soul and spirit pretty much rule our physical health?"

She slid off of the hammock and put her mug on a paint smeared shelf nearby, then turned to George. "I guess not. Now tell me what you need done while you're gone."

He grinned. ''That's the beauty of my life here. There is nothing to do. Just chill and—''

''I know, get centered.''

''That's it.'' He crossed to a wicker trunk under the high loft windows.

''Well, I've got nothing but time on my hands until the call comes from the hospital.''

''There's a fine free clinic down on Brown and—''

''That's a drug treatment center, George,'' she said. ''That's not my specialty. You know that. I work with children.''

''The only children thing I know about is the day-care center at LynTech,'' George said as he rummaged through the wicker trunk.

''A corporate institution?'' she asked with true amazement.

''No, not really. It's in LynTech, and was started for them.'' He turned with a pair of rope sandals in his hands. ''But it's changed. Lindsey Holden, the CEO's wife, has transformed it into a real community effort. It's just getting off the ground and they're taking in the children of workers in that area, anyone who needs a good day care for their child. I mean, a lot of workers in that area can't really afford expensive day care. I'm betting they'll have some kids coming in who need the kind of help you could give them.''

She was shocked that he'd mellowed to the extent that he'd give anything connected to a corporation consideration. Then again, he'd been talking a lot about LynTech since she'd arrived. ''You could be right.''

''They're even sponsoring a huge benefit next

month for the children's hospital intensive care pediatrics wing expansion. Robert Lewis, the founder of LynTech, was involved in the fund-raising, and it seemed natural to get the day-care center in on it, too. I think they're on the right track.'' He crossed to a canvas knapsack sitting by the door to the hallway. ''It was encouraging that they'd reach out like that, especially to a children's hospital. A huge fancy ball wasn't what I'd choose to raise money, but they weren't interested in any of my suggestions.''

She didn't ask what his suggestions were. ''It sounds as if their corporate heart is in the right place.''

''Who would have thought that the words *corporate* and *heart* would be in the same sentence?'' he murmured with a touch of disbelief.

''Well, that's an idea, maybe volunteering there for a week or so,'' she said, and headed into the side space where she'd set up her bed mat. ''You're leaving early?''

''Sunup,'' he said.

She stopped and looked over at him. ''Oh, speaking of corporate hearts. Mr. Ford said that he'd let them know about the cat. So, you don't need to bother telling Zane…whatever.''

''Holden, Zane Holden,'' he said. ''And speaking of Zane Holden, do you want me to give him a call and put in a good word for you at the day-care center?''

''No, thanks. I'm not sure it's a good idea anyway.'' That's all she needed was to be around people like Jack Ford all day. ''The hospital might call soon.''

"Whatever," he murmured. "Do what you think is best."

That's the way she'd always lived her life, with no strong parental rules. She'd just happened to make what she thought were good decisions. Staying clear of people like Jackson Ford was a very good decision.

Two days later, Rain gave up on a quick resolution of her position at the hospital and impulsively made a call to the day-care center at LynTech, Just For Kids. She'd spoken to a woman named Mary Garner, and Mary had been thrilled that she was interested in volunteering at the center.

Now she stood in the middle of the center, the main playroom with an awesome fantasy of a tree fashioned out of wood and paint, with tunnels in its trunk and limbs that ran from one side of the room to the other to play centers near the walls. The children were happy, and the staff seemed to be very caring. It was so much more than George had told her about.

She'd just finished a tour conducted by Mary and was taking in beautiful murals on all four walls, a ring of laughing, playing children, each with a name by them. There were maybe fifteen children in the main room right then, lying on nap mats under the sprawling wooden limbs of the play tree and soft music was being piped in. It all seemed inventive and effective.

She turned to Mary, a slightly built woman, with a cap of gray, feathery hair, and rimless glasses perched on her nose, magnifying kind blue eyes set in a softly pleasant face. She was possibly in her early sixties, spry and gentle, with a voice that matched the sweetness in her expression. Right now she was looking at Rain, and asking in a partial whisper, "So, what do you think of our lovely center?"

"I think it's terrific. Just great," she said in a voice that matched Mary's.

"I've only been here a few months, but I do love it so. And I want others to love it, too." She looked at Rain's clothes, the navy slacks and white short-sleeved sweater that she'd hoped would be suitable under the circumstances. She'd confined her hair in a single braid down her back, skimming it simply off of her face. "I'd advise that you wear more casual clothes when you're here, jeans and such. It can be hard on one's wardrobe," she said, then pressed a hand to her chest. "Oh, I'm sorry. I'm assuming far too much."

Rain didn't hesitate. She'd done this impulsively, but it had been absolutely the right thing to do. "No, you aren't. I'd love to be part of this."

Mary touched her arm. "Wonderful, wonderful, now all we have to do is take care of the formalities. Wait right here," she said and hurried off toward the office area.

Rain watched the children, enjoying the sense of peace in the space, then Mary was back with the folder Rain had brought with her containing her credentials and references. "After you called yesterday, I talked with Lindsey, Mrs. Holden, and she would be very grateful if you could help us out for a bit." She handed the packet to Rain. "We're growing so quickly and with new children coming in, we could use someone on call that could help if there was a problem."

"Well, I've got plenty of time now, but once I'm on at the hospital, any help will have to be planned around my schedule there."

"Of course. That's understood," she said. "I wonder how you heard about us."

Rain didn't need anyone's preconceived ideas about her father tainting her. As much as she loved her father, when people found out about him and his lifestyle, they automatically included her in the equation. The way Jack Ford had. She was a clinical psychologist specializing in helping troubled children. That was all the credentials she needed here.

"I actually heard about you at the hospital when I was going through the interviewing there. They're very excited about the charity ball."

"We're all very excited about it." She tapped the top of the folder in Rain's hands. "Just take that all up to Personnel and they'll give you some paperwork."

"Personnel?"

"Even though you're not getting paid, we still need you to be on staff. Insurance, I think that's what Lindsey said. The center has an office in LynTech Personnel for now. When you're through there, Mrs. Holden would like to meet you. She's in her husband's offices on the top floor. She's pregnant and been having morning sickness day and night, poor thing." Mary told her how to get to Personnel and to Zane Holden's office, then said, "Ask for Charles Gage or his assistant. They work for us. They'll be expecting you. Take the elevator just across the corridor outside the main doors."

"Okay," Rain said with a smile. "I'll see you

soon.'' Then Rain left, quietly going past the sleeping children and out the entrance doors. The main reception area was to her right, more corridors to her left, and straight across the broad, marble-floored area, was a bank of elevators. She saw a lady step into the nearest car, and she called out, ''Hold the car, please!'' as she hurried past a couple of people.

The woman, thin with short, dark hair smiled at Rain as she kept the door from closing. Rain stepped inside and pushed the button for the sixth floor. Before the door closed she saw Jack Ford walking toward the center.

This Jack Ford wasn't the same man she'd met in her ill-fated foray into the loft in the small hours of the morning. Now he was the image of what she'd labeled him that night, a corporate suit. He was in one of those suits, done in dove gray, double breasted, sleekly tailored and probably obscenely expensive, as expensive as the leather briefcase clutched in his free hand and the leather shoes on his feet. He was on a cell phone, and his face, even more sharply angular in the clear light, was set in an expression of extreme concentration. The tension in him the night before had only intensified, and she had the impression that whatever was going on right then, wasn't good.

He stopped right by the doors to the center, and closed his eyes as the elevator doors finally slid shut. She was inordinately relieved that he hadn't seen her. At least working in the center, she wouldn't have to be around him at all. There was no way they'd get involved. Her use of words shocked her slightly. Involved? He didn't even exist in the same reality she did and even more importantly, he wouldn't want to.

Chapter Three

Jack knew the cat was at the loft to stay, at least until Zane and Lindsey's lives calmed down a bit. The cat came and went as he pleased, and he only bothered with Jack when it came to food. Food ruled the cat, and the cat ruled his world as he perceived it. This morning he'd shown up and decided that it was time to eat, just as Jack was leaving the loft. Foolishly he'd gone to get the food, put it out for the cat, spilled some of the tuna on the sleeve of his jacket and had to change. All in all, it had made him more than fifteen minutes late getting to the office.

He'd barely come in the main entrance of LynTech when his cell phone rang and it was Eve. He'd been trying to make contact with her by something other than e-mail for the last two days, and now that she was on the line, he was rushed. He kept walking, and spoke into it, "Finally."

"Yes, love, finally," she said, her voice faintly tinny on the line. "I've been trying to catch you everywhere, and the cell phone number you gave me kept cutting off before it connected."

"Well, I'm on another continent," he said, nodding

to the security guard at the front, a tall, well-built man in a tailored khaki uniform.

"I know. And that's—"

A beep cut off her next word and he didn't hear it. "Eve, I've got another call coming in. Let me call you when I get to my office. Where are you?"

"At Father's."

"Okay, give me ten minutes," and he clicked over to the other call. But before he said anything, he heard a voice somewhere ahead of him. Her voice. Rain's. He couldn't make out the words, just that it was her voice, but when he looked up, he didn't see her.

He hadn't seen her again at the loft, either, and he'd thought she'd left with the old hippie for a trip. Someone on the bottom floor had said George was out of town, that he always took off like that. But for that single moment he'd been sure he'd heard her, then he'd realized how ridiculous that would have been. No one at LynTech would be walking around with bare feet, tie-dyed T-shirts or waist-length hair.

"Ford here," he said into the phone as he stopped in the corridor by a set of brightly painted doors with Just For Kids on them.

It was Martin Griggs, the negotiator for EJS with LynTech. Jack pushed the elevator call button, hoped that he wouldn't lose the signal in the car, and by the time he stepped out into the corridor, he'd forgotten about voices and was focused on business again. He assured Griggs that it wasn't anyone at the top level of LynTech who let word of the deal leak out, and by the time he got to his office, Griggs had agreed to try to get E. J. Sommers in on a conference call.

Jack hung up, and put in a call to Quint Gallagher

in New York, who was there for his son's wedding. Gallagher had known E. J. Sommers in the past and he could be an edge for them. But all he got was a voice mail service and he left a message. He hung up, went into the office they'd given him for the duration and was just taking off his jacket when Rita Donovan, executive assistant to both Zane and Matt Terrell, came into his office.

"Mr. Ford," the thin, dark haired woman said in her usual staccato voice. "I was looking for you. Mr. Holden needs to talk to you as soon as you're in."

"Okay," he said as he put his suit coat over the back of his chair. "Where is he?"

"His office. His wife's not feeling well, so he's staying with her."

"I'll be down right away," he said.

She turned to go, but stopped. "Oh, Mr. Ford, a Miss Ryder called about fifteen minutes ago. She's been trying to reach you and couldn't get through."

He'd forgotten about calling Eve back, and that bothered him. He wasn't sure why he thought it, but if he just talked to her for a while, some of the insanity that seemed to be falling into his life would disappear. "I need to call her back. Can Zane wait a few minutes?"

"I don't think so," she said.

He glanced at his watch and then at Rita. "Okay, could you call Miss Ryder and tell her I'll get back to her within the hour?" He scribbled her number in London on a sheet of paper and crossed to give it to her. "And tell her I'm sorry."

"Of course, sir," Rita said as she took the paper, then left.

Jack only took enough time to print out a file he'd e-mailed to the office earlier, before he headed for Zane's office. Once he arrived, he thought no one was there. Then he looked past the cluttered desk in the large office, into another room across the way. He didn't know what the original purpose of that room had been, but it was being used as a playroom of sorts for Zane's son, Walker.

But Walker wasn't there. Zane was with Lindsey who was all curled up on a thick mat on the floor. Zane was beside her, rubbing her back and talking softly to her. "Zane?" Jack said, hating to interrupt, but knowing they had to talk.

Zane twisted, nodded to Jack, then leaned over his wife, said something to her, kissed her quickly and stood. He came out of the room, closed the door quietly and shook his head.

"I don't know why they call it morning sickness, because she has it all the time." The rangy man was in a plain white shirt, with its long sleeves rolled up on his forearms, and navy slacks. His sandy hair was mussed as if he'd been running his fingers through it. "She had some tofu thing last night that Matt's wife, Brittany, swore would stay down. Well, it didn't," he said as he crossed to the desk. "Nothing does."

Jack always thought that Robert Lewis might have been angling to get him together with his daughter, Brittany, in the past, but despite the fact that she was beautiful, he'd avoided being anything more then friends with her. They had been around each other by default so many times, and Robert might have thought they were more than just friends. Robert was wrong. The Brittany he knew was flaky and self-centered, a woman who went through fiancées the way a lizard shed its skin. He'd probably been as shocked as Robert when she'd finally married Matt Terrell and actually settled down to her art career and a family that included a nine-year-old boy.

People changed. He knew Zane Holden had. The man he'd met before he married Lindsey, was vastly different from the one he was facing now. Business was still business, and he was good at it. But now his wife and child were his top priorities.

"I guess it's rough," he said, for lack of anything better to say about morning sickness. He couldn't begin to imagine Eve in Lindsey's condition. And it hit him that he'd never once envisioned Eve as a mother at all.

"Amen to that," Zane dropped down in his chair. He sat forward, his elbows on the piles of papers sorted on the top of the desk and looked up at Jack. "How old is the little girl you're taking care of?"

He had to think for a minute. "Four."

Zane smiled slightly. "Cute age."

Victoria was cute. Her mother had been pretty in a delicate way, and Victoria looked a lot like her mother. And Eve had said she was like a little doll. "Yes, a cute age," he said, and put the papers he'd brought with him on top of the work Zane had been doing. "I got a call from Griggs," he said, trying to get back to business and forget about why Eve and he hadn't even discussed children. "I think he's going to be able to get Sommers involved in this whole business."

"Terrific," Zane said, taking the printout Jack was offering him. "No way can we make this work with a middleman doing the talking and someone leaking the information before it's set in stone.''

''I hope he can influence Sommers.''

''Word is, little influences E. J. Sommers beyond his play toys and a good party. You'd never guess the guy was a genius.'' Zane sat back and glanced at the clock. ''Matt should be back from court soon, then we can all sit down and go through this.''

''Court?''

''Nothing serious, just clearing up some things about the adoption of Anthony. As soon as he gets back here, we'll—''

His words were cut off when Lindsey came out of the side room. Jack had seen Lindsey in February, around the time she'd found out she was pregnant and he'd thought she was pretty, in a slender, wispy way. But right then she looked miserable, her pregnancy showing despite the loose white shirt and leggings she was wearing. Her skin was as white as parchment, her eyes were smudged with shadows and an expression of discomfort etched her face.

''I'm so sorry,'' she said in a voice that was barely above a whisper. ''I know what you're doing is really important, but I can't stay here. I need to go home.''

Zane moved quickly, crossing to put his arm around her protectively and spoke in a low voice, ''That tofu was a huge mistake.''

She looked up at him, and surprisingly there was a faint smile on her pale lips. ''Now you tell me.''

He hugged her to him and spoke to Jack over her head. ''Do me a favor and cover for me here until Matt gets back from court. Let Rita know I'm going home, but I'll be back in a couple of hours?''

''No,'' Lindsey said, protesting weakly. ''I can go by myself.''

Zane acted as if she hadn't spoken and when he did, Zane saw the morning going down the tubes. ''I've got a call coming in from Tokyo,'' Zane said over his shoulder as he helped Lindsey walk to the private elevator set off to the right in the room.

''Shegata?'' Jack asked.

''Yeah. He's got information on EJS that he thinks we might be able to use.'' Zane pushed the button to go down to the parking garage and the door opened immediately. He and Lindsey got in, then he turned with his wife in his arms and looked back at Jack. ''You can work in here, and take the message. Just plug into the network. Matt should be back within the hour.''

''Take care,'' Jack said as the elevator door slid shut.

The door had just closed when the phone rang on Zane's desk. He reached for it, expecting the Japanese call, but it was Rita and she was obviously surprised to hear him answering Zane's private line.

''Mr. Ford?''

He explained about Zane and she didn't sound surprised. In fact, she said, ''I'm impressed that she lasted this long.''

Jack was impressed that Lindsey had even thought she could come into the offices in her condition. ''I'll be in here working, so send Mr. Terrell in when he arrives.''

''No problem, but I was ringing to let you know you have a call on line five. I called Miss Ryder, finally got through, and she insisted that she had to talk to you right away.''

He didn't like the feeling he was getting. Eve usually respected business, no matter what. ''Put her through,'' he said.

The next thing he knew, Eve was on the line, that breathy voice, the slight pout in her tone. It was good to hear her voice again, but he'd been right to feel that something had to be wrong when she started with, ''I'm sorry to have to insist on talking to you, but things on this end are in a mess.''

He glanced at the clock. It was late at night in London. His stomach tightened. ''Is something wrong with Victoria?''

''Not with the girl, exactly. It's Mrs. Ferris.''

Jack hadn't had an e-mail from the woman this morning and had actually been relieved after ploughing through three or four every day since he'd left. ''What is it?''

''Her sister's having an operation and she's the only one who can help her. She gave notice that she's taking off very soon. She's in quite a tizzy and you need a new nanny.''

He was actually relieved when she got to the bottom line. A new nanny? He didn't like the idea of Victoria having to get used to another nanny so soon, but Eve would be there and it wouldn't be for more than a few weeks. ''Okay, as long as you're there, a new nanny isn't the end of the world.''

''It's not that simple, love.''

He closed his eyes and exhaled. ''Then tell me why not?''

''I'm not going to be here myself.''

''What?''

''Well, I was bored without you here, and Sonny and Lex asked me to go to their place in Acapulco. They're expecting me and they made plans. I thought that since Mexico is close to Texas, I could go down there, get some relaxation, then when you're done there, you could fly down to meet me and well...''

This wasn't going to be as easy as he'd hoped. ''What about Victoria?''

''Well, there's no way she can go along with me, nanny or not. I mean, Sonny and Lex have those horrid little dogs and I don't think any of them like children. But, don't worry. The service that sent Mrs. Ferris says they don't have one for a permanent position at this time, but they can send temporary staff, maybe for a day or two at a time, and they said they'll be sure that someone will always be here.''

He'd thought that going on holiday was to include Victoria, but if she was in London with a round-robin of baby-sitters, Eve in Acapulco and him here...no, that wouldn't work. He couldn't do it. This wasn't what he'd promised Ian and Jean at all. ''What do they mean, someone will always be there, moving around every day or two? What are we talking about, nanny musical chairs?''

She laughed, a throaty sound that jarred him. He wasn't trying to be funny. ''Oh, love, don't be ridiculous.''

Ridiculous was a child being cared for by different people every day. ''Isn't there someone who can be with Victoria for the full time, then fly her over for the vacation?''

''Well, there is a nanny that the Kents had a few

years ago, but they didn't keep her long. She's okay, but they didn't like her all that well. But she'd probably do in a pinch.''

He wasn't going to pawn Victoria off on some nanny who was sub par, and it bothered him that Eve thought that was even an option. ''No, that won't do.''

He heard Eve's exasperated sigh. ''Well, Mrs. Ferris says she has to be out of here in three or four days at the latest, so what choice do you have? Oh, I know, your mother!''

That idea never even saw the light of day with him. ''No, not Mother.'' She was busy somewhere in Italy, and she had barely responded to his situation with Victoria. ''Get a good nanny,'' had been all she'd said. He knew that when his father had passed away, she'd been stunned, but determined to keep living the life she wanted to live. He'd made sure she could, but he never looked to her as a source of support for him. He'd never known a time when she'd been strong or independent. And nothing had changed in the past ten years.

''Then what do you want?'' Eve asked.

He'd never thought of himself as chauvinistic, but right then, he really wanted Eve to say she'd stay with Victoria and be there for her until they could meet for a vacation. But he knew that wasn't going to happen. Part of him worried that their marriage would not exactly be smooth sailing. Right now, the only options he had were to have Victoria stranded in London with another stranger or the option he knew he had to choose. He took a breath then said words that he barely had time to measure. "Bring her here on your way to Mexico."

"What?" Eve sounded shocked, as if he'd told her to walk on water.

"You're flying to Acapulco, so make a stopover in Houston and bring her with you."

She laughed again, but this time there was little humor in it. It was more nervous disbelief. "Are you bonkers? How can you take care of her and do your job?"

He didn't have a clue, but he said, "I'll work it out. Just get Mrs. Ferris to pack Victoria's things, then let me know when your flight arrives."

"Okay," she murmured. "But what about our holiday after you're done there?"

He couldn't even think about that. "We'll work it out."

"I'll hold you to that," she said softly. "I've missed you."

"I've missed you, too." Suddenly the idea of Eve in Houston was very tempting. If she could stay over a day or so, to get Victoria settled and to spend time with him, that wouldn't be all bad. "Let me know when you're arriving."

"We'll try to get out of here in three days. And, Jack?"

He had things to do, and his mood shifted. He wanted to get off the phone and get on with things. "Yes?"

"I love you."

He closed his eyes again. "I know."

"No, love, you're supposed to say, 'I love you, too.' If you love me."

He exhaled and felt the tension building inside him. "Love you," he said.

"No, say, 'I, Jack, love you, Eve,' the way most fiancées would do."

"Eve, not now," he said tightly.

"Okay," she said. "I can wait."

He exhaled. "Call?"

"Sure. As soon as I know. Now I have to make the child understand what's going on. Not that I think she understands much of anything. But I'll try…just for you."

Victoria understood, he didn't doubt that. She just didn't react to anything. He wished there was some way to get into her mind to see what was going on. "You're terrific."

"Absolutely, and remember that," Eve said, then the line went dead.

He slowly hung up, and tried to figure out where to start. Zane was gone, Matt hadn't shown up yet. Rita. He could ask her about nannies or baby-sitters. She seemed to be indispensable to both Matt and Zane. Maybe she could find someone to step in and be with Victoria, and possibly get something set up in the loft for the little girl. If he had to, he'd move to another place, as long as he could be hooked up to the office wherever he went.

He turned to go and find Rita, but stopped in his tracks, stunned to see Rain standing in the open door of Zane's office, watching him. It was as if the thought of the loft had conjured her up, making her materialize not more then ten feet away from him. But he could see her breathing, could almost catch a hint of that flowery essence that clung to her. She was very real.

Rain. With her hair sleekly pulled back form her finely boned face, exposing how large her eyes were, he could see a faint suggestion of freckles dusting her small nose. She was in tailored dark slacks, an almost prim white top and—he looked down—no bare feet. White dress sandals. Even without her tie-dyed T-shirt and loose hair, she didn't look as if she belonged here at all.

Rain faced Jack Ford from the doorway to Zane Holden's office, and knew that his shock at seeing her had been as great as her shock seeing him moments ago. She'd expected Lindsey Holden, a woman who had almost attained sainthood in the eyes of the people she'd just talked to. Even the personnel man had almost waxed poetic about how much the woman had done for the day-care center.

But it wasn't Lindsey she was facing now. It was the man she'd heard on the phone moments earlier, his back to her, speaking in a low voice. She'd watched the way his shoulders tested the fine fabric of his silky shirt when he took a breath, then said, "Love you." They must have been said to his fiancée, but they were said with something of a throw-away. As if they weren't nearly as important to him as they should be.

Now he was looking right at her. Actually, he was looking her over. From her head to her feet, then back to her face, and she couldn't begin to read his thoughts. She hated it when a person was so closed that you had to guess at what they were thinking and feeling.

"You," he said.

"You," she repeated, tipping her head slightly to one side.

He came toward her, meeting her gaze, his eyes dark, but with flashes of gold in the irises. "You have got to be the quietest person in the world," he muttered. "I didn't hear you come in."

"You were too busy talking." She didn't mention that she hadn't knocked, or that she'd just stood there and listened to him when she'd known she should have just left. "But at least you aren't carrying a weapon this time."

He shrugged. "I didn't have any warning. Now, what on earth are you doing here?" he asked, as if she was an alien.

She wanted to say, "None of your business," but there was a tension in his face that stopped her. If he really was in trouble with the company, that would definitely account for some of his rudeness. "I was looking for Lindsey Holden."

"You're out of luck. Mrs. Holden's gone." He frowned at her. "You don't work here, do you?"

He was using the same tense tone he'd used with his fiancée moments ago, and she didn't like it one bit. "What do you think?"

"I just asked," he said.

"No, I don't work here and you're nothing if you aren't predictable."

"What does that mean?"

"Still judging people, aren't you?"

"I'm not judging anyone."

"Oh, you aren't? Aren't you thinking, no corporation would hire me, not when I'm a... What did you call me? Oh, yes, a hippie."

"I never said anything like that," he countered without missing a beat.

"You did that night. And you're probably thinking it now. And all because of George." She shook her head. "Oh, you are such a snob."

"And you jump to every conclusion but the right one," he muttered.

"Do I?"

"What are you here for?"

"Don't worry, I'm not here to go after someone about corporate greed or plundering the rain forests, or peddling incense and granola."

"Really?" he murmured with a raised eyebrow.

If he hadn't been so annoying, she would have told him exactly why she was here. Instead, she said, "No, actually, I'm here to give uptight, stressed-out, humorless executives lessons in chilling out, getting centered and getting in touch with their inner selves."

He laughed then, but it was devoid of humor. "Oh, sure, now who's doing the labeling?"

She made herself smile slightly. "I never said I was talking about you, but if the stress fits..." She shrugged. "Well, what can I say?"

His mouth thinned. "Who made you the one to teach anyone how to relax?"

The phone behind him rang before Rain could get herself in any deeper with the man. "I have to take this," he said and crossed to the desk to answer it. "Yes?" He listened. "Okay, Rita, tell Mr. Shegata that I'm going to be the one talking to him, then put him through."

He glanced back at Rain, covered the mouthpiece with his free hand and said, "If I ever need lessons in relaxing, I'll be sure to call you."

"Sure, any time. But don't wait too long. You look ready to self-destruct."

His expression darkened again, but he never got to respond.

"Mr. Holden?" someone said from behind Rain and she saw the thin lady who had held the elevator door for her, stepping around her and going into the office. "Mr. Ford," she said. "He'll be on in a minute."

"Is Mr. Terrell back yet?"

"No, sir. Is there anything else I can help you with?" she asked him, not even looking at Rain.

"Just let Mr. Terrell know that the call came through when he shows up."

"Yes, sir."

"And, Rita—I need to talk to you as soon as I get this call done."

"I'll be at my desk," she said, then looked at Rain. "Can I help you?"

"I was looking for Mrs. Holden, but I'll catch her later." She glanced at Jack. "I'm leaving."

"You're done?" he asked, still on hold for his call.

She looked right at him and said, "For now. But if you want those lessons, you know where I live." And she left. As she headed for the outer door, she could have sworn she heard Jack start to speak in Japanese. She'd come to meet Lindsey Holden and ended up in an argument with Jack Ford.

She'd always believed in fate, that nothing was an accident in this life, but right then she wondered what on earth good it could do for her to argue with an uptight executive who thought she was some crazy, free spirit. He didn't bother to find out who or what she really was, and she'd never know why he was like he was. That bothered her, too. Or why the things others had thought about her over the years, things she'd passed off with little more than a shrug, stung coming from him.

If she ever saw him again, if she ever ran into him here or at the loft, she'd be nice and she wouldn't let things deteriorate the way they had just now. The man was as tight as a coiled spring, obviously intense about his work. And she didn't want to add to that tension. She'd been sarcastic when she'd offered to give him lessons in relaxing, but on some level she meant it. Not that he'd ever take her up on it.

Chapter Four

The cat was driving Jack nuts. He wouldn't eat the food in the loft, and he wouldn't leave Jack alone. He crawled over the computer, hitting random keys, jumped off the wall at Jack more than once, and his hair was everywhere. "Keep him there for now," Zane had said. "Lindsey is too sick to have him at home." Jack had agreed, but right now he thought if the damn cat made one more sneak attack, Lindsey Holden wouldn't have to worry about the cat any longer. He'd be gone.

Jack sat back in the chair, stretched his arms over his head and turned away from the computer just after ten in the evening. He felt painful tension in his neck and shoulders and for a fleeting moment thought of Rain's description of him as uptight, stressed out, and a humorless executive. He pushed that memory away, and stood.

If things didn't work out soon, he'd be more than uptight. The nanny situation for Victoria, who was arriving the next day, was hopeless. The best Rita could do was get a baby-sitter on call. Zane encouraged him to use the day-care center and although he'd

fought that idea, he was beginning to realize that
might be his only option for the bulk of Victoria's
care. The loft wasn't right for a child, but moving
wouldn't make it easy to stay connected. Nothing was
going right. And that wasn't even considering the EJS
acquisition negotiations, which were rocky at best.

He crossed to the long, iron-framed window to one
side of the computer desk, the window that doubled
as an emergency exit to the fire escape. He pulled it
back and felt the coolness of the May night against
his skin, then stepped up and out onto the metal landing. They'd eventually find the leak that started the
chain reaction of problems with the acquisition, but
right now he felt helpless. It was like watching a train
wreck in slow motion. Not a great way to fill his days
and nights, and the longer he was here, the more complicated things got. The high-tech division of EJS that
they were after was perfect for LynTech and no one
wanted to give up on it.

He felt Joey brush past his legs, then saw the cat
go silently up the metal stairs that led to the roof. The
next instant he was gone. "Stupid cat," Jack muttered
as he turned to go back inside, but stopped when he
saw someone on the fire escape of the next loft. Rain.

She was sitting absolutely still on the landing, her
hair loose and flowing down her back, dressed in that
skimpy T-shirt and her face lifted to the starry heavens. Each hand was resting on her knees, palms up.
The only sounds were the hum of the city in the distance and the occasional car horn. Moonlight bathed
her in a silvery glow, and he could barely make out
her breathing. He just watched, wondering how some-

one could drive him so crazy, yet radiate such peace that it almost made him ache.

When Jack realized that just watching her had brought another ache to him, that his thoughts of peace had been pushed aside by the sight of her delicate beauty, the way her throat arched, and her breasts rose and fell with each measured breath, he made himself turn to go back inside. But before he could touch the window frame, she startled him by calling out, "Can't sleep?"

He'd thought she had no idea he was there, and wondered how long she'd known he was watching her. "Just getting some fresh air," he called back.

She never moved from her gazing at the heavens, but said, "Trouble?"

"What?"

"I heard you were in a heap of trouble with the business, and I thought that might be keeping you awake. All that tension and worry."

She never stopped. "I don't sleep much," he said.

"I bet you don't." That was when she moved, rocking forward, and getting to her feet in one smooth motion. She turned, laid something on the metal railing and looked across at him. She was slender and delicate in the moonlight, her hair tumbling down her back and her features softly shadowed. "You know, meditation really could help."

"So could a handful of sleeping pills," he muttered.

"What was that?"

"I need to get back to work."

"Me, too," she said, moving her hand and sending the item she'd placed on the railing spiraling down into the darkness below. She reached for it and for a split second he thought she was going to fall right after it the way she tipped forward.

"No! Stop!" he yelled, and he was heady with relief when she straightened up, completely safe and secure on the landing.

"Oh, shoot," she said, looking down into the distant alley. "I can't believe I did that." She reached toward the release for the stairs that were lowered in emergencies.

"What are you doing?" he asked.

"Going down to get it."

He looked down into the darkness, and found himself saying, "Oh, no you don't. Wait until morning to get it."

She turned back to him again. "Oh, sure, and by then some drunks will have my journal and be sharing it over a bottle of cheap wine."

"It's not safe to go down there." He motioned around them. "This isn't exactly a good neighborhood."

"I've lived in worse," she said. "And I'm getting my book."

"I won't let you," he said.

She darted him a look and he was sort of glad he wasn't close enough to see it too clearly. "You won't *let* me?"

He reached for the release for his emergency stairs. "Just sit tight, and I'll go down and get it for you," he said, without giving her a chance to argue. The stairs slid down to within three feet of the ground, and he hurried down them. He jumped the final distance and as his eyes adjusted, he spotted the book lying near the wall. He picked it up, then looked up at Rain on her fire escape where she was haloed by the partial moon. ''Got it.''

''Terrific,'' she said and hit her release button on her stairs. He climbed up to her on the landing, and held out the book to her. She took it, hugging it to her breast, then grinned at him in the moonlight. The expression jolted him. It was one of pure pleasure. ''Thank you so much. You're a real hero.''

''I doubt rescuing a book is enough to be dubbed a hero,'' he murmured.

''Well, I think it is,'' she said and turned to the deep window she'd come out of. ''And it warrants something special.''

He watched her start in through the open window, then she paused and looked back at him. ''Well, come on.''

He hesitated, the idea of being with her longer a bit too tempting, and he knew he should just leave. But knowing what he should do and doing it were obviously two different things. Instead of saying, ''Thanks, but no thanks,'' he found himself going after her and stepping into the other loft.

He stopped as his feet hit the hardwood floor and looked around at candles everywhere, the scent of incense in the air mixed with an overlay of oil paint and thinner...and chaos. The loft had no rhyme or reason to it in any sense of the words.

The center was scattered with art in various stages of completion. At least what some might call art. To him it was paint thrown at canvases and left to dry, done in brilliant primary colors. Stacked canvases leaned against partial walls, tarps protected part of the wooden floors, and the overhead lights were heavy banks of bulbs that mercifully weren't lit at the moment. He thought it would be blinding if they ever went on all at once. A rope hammock hung from the overhead beams dead in the middle of the chaos.

He glanced at Rain who disappeared into a side space. "Drink?" she called back to him.

He could use one. "Sure."

"Anything special?"

"Whatever you have," he said, and as he glanced to the left, he grimaced slightly at the sight of a side space with a mattress pad on the floor, a huge king-size thing, with tangled blankets and sheets and tons of pillows piled at the head. He looked away, hating where his mind was going, and as he turned, Rain was there.

"It'll just be a minute," she said, then reached past him and grabbed two huge pillows covered with flag material. "Sit. Relax," she said as she tossed one to the floor right behind him.

He hesitated, and she touched him, just the tips of her fingers on his shoulders, then she pushed and he tumbled back onto the pillow. It whooshed slightly as he made impact, then he was in the softness, trying to right himself into a reasonable sitting position. Meanwhile she'd put the other pillow behind her, then gracefully lowered herself onto it and tucked her legs under her. The T-shirt barely covered her thighs.

She studied him for a long moment, then said, "So, why couldn't you sleep?"

"I never said I couldn't sleep. I actually haven't tried to sleep. I was working."

She cocked her head to one side and clicked her

tongue. "This time of night, and you weren't trying to sleep?"

"It's only ten o'clock, and you weren't sleeping, either," he pointed out.

"Of course not. I was meditating."

"Of course."

She stood in one fluid motion when a high-pitched whistling started. "Just a minute," she said, hurrying past him.

The next thing he knew, she was there again, offering him a heavy ceramic mug. "Here you go. This should help you relax."

He almost said he didn't need to relax, but that would have been a complete lie. He took the mug, felt the heat radiate into his hands, and he looked down into swirling liquid that reflected the flicker of candle light. "What is this?"

"Camomile tea. Great for frayed nerves, tension, stress. And it'll help you sleep."

He looked up at her standing over him, and as tiny as she was, she was towering over him now. "Don't you have anything with alcohol?"

"Good grief," she said, sitting back down and facing him, cradling her own cup of tea. "You don't need alcohol to relax. That's self-defeating. Alcohol numbs you, it doesn't relax you."

Numbing wouldn't be so bad. "It sounded like a good idea," he murmured, staring at the green tea.

"Sip it," she said and took a drink of her own tea. She smiled slightly and sighed. "It's so soothing. Really helps."

He cautiously took a sip and it wasn't too bad. Not good, but not too bad. "It's okay."

"I thought being English and all, you'd be very used to tea."

"I'm not English. I just live there for now."

"Hmmm, I wondered why your accent was so—" she shrugged "—thin, I guess."

"Thin?"

"Well, you know, sometimes you can't even understand someone from England, with all the strange words and the accent."

He understood. "You get used to it."

She put her tea on the floor, then stood and was coming around behind him. Before he knew what she was doing, she was kneeling behind him and her hands touched his shoulders. He tensed even more. "What are you doing?"

"Shhh," she said, her fingers pressing into the muscles to the sides of his neck. "You are so tight." Her fingers pressed into the muscles, not giving pain, but making it impossible for him to even think clearly. "Just let me try some accupressure."

"What?" he asked, turning to look at her.

"Pressure points," she said, reaching for his mug of tea and putting it off to one side before she touched him again. "They control the actions of the muscles, and if you hit them just right—" she pressed her fingers into a spot on either side of his neck "—like right here, you can make the muscles relax. It's remarkable."

Her touch was remarkable and he could literally feel his muscles relaxing. Her fingers kneaded his muscles, making a pattern along his shoulders, back to his neck, then pushed into his spine between his shoulder blades. He'd had massages before, but none of them had been like this. His head lolled forward, his eyes closed and her hands eased toward his arms, pressing, kneading, finding spots in his muscles that almost burned, then eased.

And for a startling moment, he knew that her touch was working magic. Tension was seeping away. He exhaled in a rush, letting it happen, letting go, until she whispered in his ear, "That's it, let go, just relax, let it ease out of you." She was so close that he felt her warm breath brush his ear, her voice seducing him all over again.

His response in the dream had been so very basic, and that hadn't changed. Tension came with it, and whatever he'd been able to let go of because of her touch, was back. His body responded of its own accord, and he moved quickly to stop the madness that he knew was coming. He put his hands over hers on his shoulders and stopped them from moving. "Enough," he said, pushing himself to his feet to take a deep steadying breath before he turned to her. "That's enough."

She was slowly standing, looking up at him, her rich brown eyes narrowed on him, her head tilted slightly to one side. He couldn't tell if she knew what she'd done to him, or not. "Are you sure?" she asked.

"Yes," he muttered, feeling more than foolish.

"Too bad. It was working," she said with a shrug.

It had been working, okay, but not the way she thought. Not when he was so very aware of her. Her silvery hair, her bare thighs, and that thing on her slender ankle. He must have been staring, because she said, "It's a promise anklet." He looked up at her, and met her gaze. "It's woven from hand spun yarn and it's given as a promise."

"What kind of promise?" he said.

She shrugged. "Someone gives it to someone else to promise they'll always be there for them. That they'll never forget to remember them."

His stomach knotted. "Like an engagement?"

She actually laughed at that, tossing her head back as the warm sound filled the air for a long moment. "Oh, goodness, no. Nothing like that. George gave it to me. He made it himself."

The knot grew a bit and tension was back full force, worse than it had been when he came into this loft. "Oh, of course. An engagement is a commitment, isn't it?"

Her laughter died completely. "What are you talking about?"

"You and George. Here."

"I don't understand."

"What's this setup called? Going with the flow? His karma fitting yours? Make love not war?"

"You think…?" She put both hands on her hips, and a smile started to tease at her mouth and eyes. "Oh, good grief, you're really a piece of work, aren't you?"

He was more then ready to leave. "Forget it."

"No, I won't." Her chin lifted slightly. "Not that I have to, but let me define my relationship with George."

He didn't want that any more than he'd wanted that horrible tea. What a mistake it had been to come here. "No, you don't have to," he muttered. "I need to get back to my place and do some work."

She didn't move, standing between him and the door. To get around her, he would have had to weave his way between paintings, unfinished canvases and more pillows stacked around them. "You know, I hate people believing things about me that aren't true." She came a step closer, bringing a wave of flowery scent with her. She barely came to his chin, but that didn't stop her from tipping her head and looking him right in the eye. "Especially uptight, rigid—"

"Enough of that," he muttered, holding up both hands, palms out toward her.

She exhaled and he could see her shoulders tremble slightly with the action. "Okay, fair enough." Stopping the massage hadn't lessened that awareness he had of her. It had a life of its own, and almost made it impossible for him to breathe when he saw the fullness of her bottom lip, the slight sharpness to her chin, the arch of her neck. "This is George's loft, his artwork, his life. He's a good, decent person, who truly believes in his causes. He wants to save the world, as corny as that sounds. He always has. He'll never change, and to be honest, I don't want him to. That's why I love him."

The knot was almost painful in his middle now. "Great." He would have left then, getting to the door any way he had to, but he never had a chance to try because she touched him again. A light contact on his forearm with just the tips of her fingers, and for an instant he hated George. He hated the idea of her loving him, and defending him with so much passion. George touching her, and her touch on him. "What?"

"The bottom line?" she asked.

She kept the contact between them. "Is there a bottom line?" he breathed.

"Damn it, yes." There was no smile on her face now. "You make things so damn hard. Don't you ever loosen up and just go with the flow, just let life be what it is and stop fighting it every inch of the way?"

"I don't need lectures from you about how I deal with life," he replied as he stared down at her. He watched the way her nostrils flared with each breath she took, inhaled that scent hovering in the air, and he felt a need that he wouldn't even put a name to starting to build in him.

"You could be doing damage to your heart," she said softly.

"Are you admitting that I do have a heart?"

Her touch shifted from his arm, to his chest, where she pressed the palm of her hand to his heart. He felt the warmth of her touch through the thin material of his shirt. "Oh, yes, you have a heart," she whispered.

If he'd left right then, he would have been free and clear of whatever spell she could weave around him. But he didn't leave. He just stood there while her hand made a slow circle around his heart. Her dark eyes looked into his, and he didn't move. Her tongue touched her full bottom lip, and he didn't move. She exhaled softly, and he still didn't move.

Her hand stilled on him, pressing to his heart, and all he could do was say, "I need to..." What? Run? Get out of here?

"Yes," she whispered, "you need something."

He knew then what he needed, what he'd probably needed since hearing her voice drifting to him in his dreams. He wasn't running. He wasn't escaping, he was moving closer, and finally, his mouth found her softly parted lips.

Rain knew it was coming. She could feel it in the air around them as soon as she touched him, as soon as she felt his heart beating against her palm. Yet, when he kissed her, it stunned her. Almost as much as her reaction to the contact stunned her. Her immediate response was to open herself to him, to get closer, close enough to feel his heart against hers, instead of against her hand. To blend with him, to lose the line of differentiation between them. Something she'd never wanted or craved before.

But nothing about her reactions to Jackson Ford were normal or usual for her. Not the hostility that seemed to spring up between them when she had never fought with anyone in her life before. Or an awareness even in the hostility that made her feel more alive than she had a right to feel. When his lips found hers, when she felt his heat and need, ''normal'' had no basis in her actions. She'd never been one for ''free love,'' or being promiscuous, no matter what people thought of her. That wasn't what she was about, but at that moment, she didn't care that she barely knew this man, or that he was everything that she'd never wanted in a man. Except for that wrenching need that made her want to get closer and closer to him.

Then suddenly and completely, the contact was gone. He was pushing her back, taking a step away from her, and when she opened her eyes, he was staring at her.

"Boy," she whispered and touched her lips with the tips of her fingers. "Boy, oh boy, oh boy."

He didn't say a thing. He just took another step back, then turned away from her and headed for the door. She didn't turn to see him open the door, and she couldn't stop herself from calling after him, "If you let yourself go, no telling what you'd do, Mr. Ford." Then the door closed with a firm click and he was gone.

"Stupid, stupid, stupid," she muttered to herself, closing her eyes so tightly that colors exploded behind her lids. A man like that. A suit. Everything that she'd been brought up to find dishonor in, that was him. And he was engaged to money and proper wealth and elegance. On top of that, the idiot thought she was shacking up with George. Then she'd let him kiss her.

If she hadn't felt so confused, she would have laughed out loud. But there wasn't much humor left in her. She opened her eyes, quickly picked up the two mugs of tea from the floor, but on her way to the kitchen area, a knock sounded on her door. It couldn't be Jack. It shouldn't be Jack. And George had still been on the Coast when he called less than two hours ago.

She put the mugs down on the nearest table that held all of George's canvas cutting tools, then padded over to the door. "Who is it?" she called.

"Jack."

She closed her eyes again, took a breath, braced herself, then opened her eyes and opened the door. "What?" she asked, more abruptly than she meant to.

''My door's locked,'' he said, his expression tinged with frustration. ''I left through the window.''

''Oh, sure, I forgot.''

''So did I,'' he muttered as he went past her to head toward her fire escape exit. ''Sorry for the inconvenience,'' he said without looking back at her. He reached the window and stepped out into the night. She went after him, and by the time she was on the fire escape, he had the stairs down and was climbing toward the alleyway.

She watched him almost disappear into the deep shadows below, then he was climbing up the steps on his fire escape and she pulled her ladder back up and locked it. The man was so controlled it made her teeth ache. No mention of the kiss. Not even an apology. Not even a, ''Boy was that a horrible mistake for me.'' Nothing, and here she was, filled with turmoil. And he just put it behind him. He got onto his landing and pulled his stairs back up.

When he turned in her direction, she spoke without thinking, needing to make some sense out of what had just happened. ''What was that all about?'' she called over to him.

''I told you, I got locked out, and—''

''No, I didn't mean that. I meant you kissing me.''

He was motionless for a long moment, then he said, ''That shouldn't have ever happened.''

''Why?''

''First, I'm engaged.''

That was a given, but it still raised heat in her face. ''Secondly?''

She could hear him exhale as he gripped the metal rail of the fire escape. ''Pick your reason. You think

I'm some uptight conservative, and you're…'' His voice trailed off.

''I'm what?''

''Whatever,'' he muttered.

That was it. Whatever. She was whatever she was. What he thought she was, at least. Beneath him. Not good enough for him. Some strange hippie. She finally found anger, and she clung to it, because it made sense. The rest of what she'd been feeling didn't make any sense at all. She hugged her arms around herself to stop a vague trembling starting deep inside her. ''Yeah, whatever. You're engaged and I'm a hippie. And don't forget to add that you're a grade-A snob.''

He held up both hands, palms out toward her. ''Let's stop this. You've got George and your life, and I've got Eve and my life.''

''Sure, you've got your fiancée and I've got my George,'' she said, as he turned to go into the other loft.

She saw him push his window back, but before he went inside, she called after him again. ''Oh, by the way, not that it matters, but George is my father.''

Chapter Five

Jack stopped, took a breath, and the words hung in the air between them. He turned, not at all certain what he thought he heard her yell after him. She was still where she'd been, by the rail, staring at him, hugging herself. Not moving. Had he hallucinated that? No. She'd said that George Armstrong was her father, but he had to hear it again. "What did you say?"

"George is my father," she said very clearly this time.

"Your father?" He gripped the cold metal of the railing in front of him.

"Listen carefully and grasp this concept, he's my father, my dad, my parent. And my father is visiting my mother in Palo Alto on the Coast right now. And I'm staying with him until I get a place of my own."

Not some middle-aged hippie lover? His relief was staggering and so very out of line. It shouldn't matter to him, not any more than the kiss should. But he couldn't shake the relief that was filtering through him. "Why didn't you say something before this?"

"Because it was none of your business," she said, tossing his own words back at him.

She was right, it wasn't. It meant nothing, despite the way the knot in his middle dissolved. "I didn't think—"

"No, you didn't think, did you?" she said cutting him off. "But forget it. Forget all of this. You're right. You're engaged and I'm a hippie, and it doesn't matter a bit that I'm not shacking up with George. But I hate people believing things about me that aren't true. And you tend to do that all the time."

His hands were gripping the rail so tightly that the metal was cutting into his palms. "If I don't have the facts, I—"

"Jump to conclusions," she muttered, but he heard her very distinctly through the night air. Then she said more loudly, "Forget it. It doesn't matter."

He knew that was lie, but he didn't want to stand there and argue, or even try to figure out the truth. He pushed that thought away. She'd given him his out by saying it didn't matter, and he took it. "You're right, it doesn't matter," he said.

She stared at him, then without a word, she turned and was gone. He heard her window click shut. He was alone. The night was balmy and soft around him, but he felt chilled. He went inside, turned to close the window, but wasn't fast enough. The cat sprang out of the night, and in through the opening. Jack closed the window, and when he turned, the animal was sitting there, staring at him.

"What?" he asked with frustration, no more able to read the cat's mind than he'd been able to read Rain's. And maybe he didn't want to. He never wanted to know what she really thought. The cat was easier to guess at. He probably had the mantra going on inside him, "I hate you, but I want food. Give me food. Give me food." The cat moved then, jumping to the floor and heading for the kitchen. Jack followed him. "How predictable," he muttered. "Food." He opened a can of cat food and laid it on the floor for the cat who crossed to it, sniffed it, then looked up at him.

"That's all I've got," he said. "If you want dolphin-free tuna, go next door."

Joey looked back at the food, then began to eat it. Jack went into the living area, ignored the work area, turned out the lights, and headed to the bedroom. He stripped, showered, then got into bed. Before long, the cat had joined him. He didn't get too close, but lay near Jack's side. "You don't mind some uptight, humorless suit?" he asked.

The cat purred, and Jack closed his eyes ready to sleep. But sleep didn't come. And not because of work worries. Every time he closed his eyes, he saw Rain. He remembered her touching him, the easing in him, then the rush of tension. He saw himself kissing Rain, and he felt that same sense of losing control he'd had the moment he'd kissed her. He finally got up, and went out into the main space.

He glanced to where Rita's assistant had put a rollaway bed for Victoria, partitioning it with a folding screen. At least the child would have a bed when she got here tomorrow. He'd meet the flight at the airport, talk to Eve and maybe she'd stay for a while. He needed that. He needed that badly. With her, he knew where he stood, and he knew what to expect. Eve was a world of difference from Rain. Hell, they weren't even in the same universe.

THE CONFERENCE ROOM at LynTech was tense the next morning. It was filled with all of the decision makers for the corporation, either in person or on satellite feed. Jack sat to the right of Zane and faced Matt Terrell across the long, polished table. Even Robert Lewis was sitting in on the conference as a consultant. He sat back farther in his chair, caught Robert's eye and the older man nodded to him, then looked at the big screen on the far wall.

Jack followed his gaze and saw Benton Ames on a satellite hookup from New York. "The way we see it, the leak about the negotiations came from Houston, but that's as specific as we can get. We're in for a rough ride."

Tension knotted in the back of Jack's neck and he spoke up. "Okay, what now?"

Zane glanced at Jack. "I've got a few things in motion, but so far, there isn't a trail to follow." He looked at Robert Lewis. "Sir? Any ideas?"

The older man shrugged. "Hunt the traitor down like a dog, and kill him on the spot," he muttered. The room went dead silent, then Robert smiled, "Or fire them. Whichever you all think is appropriate."

There was nervous laughter from a few, then Zane stood. "On that note, we need a break. Benton, hold on and we'll take ten, okay?"

The man in New York agreed. Jack stood and Robert was there by him, resting his hand on Jack's shoulder. "No smile for my very small attempt at levity?" he asked.

Jack didn't feel much like smiling at all. "It's a mess, Robert."

"But it's business, and you're taking it too personally. You need to remember that."

If the older man said to relax and get centered, he knew he'd lose it. But Robert didn't. Jack exhaled. "I thought this acquisition with EJS was a slam dunk, that it would be over and done before the rest of the world knew what hit them. I just never expected something like this."

"In this business, if they smell blood, they're like sharks," Robert said. "They know that EJS is vulnerable at the moment, and they're jumping into the fray." He exhaled. "I've done the same thing myself before."

"Mr. Ford?"

Jack turned and saw Rita heading toward him. She'd been recruited to meet Eve's flight and take Eve and Victoria to the loft when he'd been trapped in this meeting. "Did you get things taken care of?" he asked.

"I hate to do this when we've got such problems around here, but—"

"Their flight was canceled?" he asked abruptly.

"Oh, no, they landed on time, safe and sound. That's not the problem."

"Then what is the problem?"

"You'd better come with me for a minute," she said and led the way to a side room. She stopped and motioned to her left.

Jack stopped when he saw Victoria, sitting primly on a chair facing the entrance, all dressed up in a navy pinafore, white tights and black patent leather shoes.

She clutched the old doll to her chest and simply stared up at him. Eve was nowhere in sight, and he turned to Rita. "What's going on here?"

She motioned to Victoria. "She couldn't stay at the loft alone, and I can't be gone from the office any longer, not today of all days."

"What do you mean, alone? Where's Miss Ryder?"

"On her way to Mexico, I presume. That's the problem. She had to get going, because her connecting flight was canceled and she had to take what she could get, so she left to make arrangements. She told me to take care of Victoria, so I brought her here." She shrugged. "What now?"

He'd been informed, just before the meeting, that the nanny Rita had found couldn't take over with Victoria for at least two more days. By then Eve and Victoria had been long gone from London and on their way here. He'd hoped to see Eve, and rid himself of any frustration. He'd thought together, they could work this out, but that wasn't going to happen. "I can't leave the meeting, and we're going to dive right into work when it's over. Any ideas?"

"Well, I can't watch her. I mean, I would if I could, she's a sweet little thing, but it was tight with me leaving at all to get her. How about someone at the loft, a neighbor or some one you know?"

That was out of the question. "There is no one. Do you know of any baby-sitting service or something like that to take up the slack at least for today."

"There's the day-care center here at LynTech."

"No, I think a babysitter would be better."

"I don't know of any, but I could call the nanny agency and see if they have emergency help?"

He nodded. "Do it."

"Yes, sir." She looked at Victoria who sat staring intently at her doll, in silence. "I guess she can sit in my office while I make the call."

Zane came to the door of the conference room. "We're back, Jack." He spotted Victoria and came into the side room. "Is this your little girl?"

Jack nodded. "Yes, she just arrived."

Zane came across to where Victoria sat and dropped to his haunches in front of her. "Hello there, my name's Zane. What's yours?"

She looked at Zane with wide eyes, then suddenly moved, getting off the chair and hurrying over to where Jack stood. She stopped right beside him, not touching him, but getting as close as she could without making contact.

"Her name's Victoria," Jack said, touching her head.

"Nice to meet you, Miss Victoria," Zane said as he stood, then looked at Jack. "Are you ready?"

He looked at Rita, and the woman took the cue. She reached for Victoria, and although the little girl didn't hold on to her, she let Rita take her hand. "We'll be in my office for now," she said and Victoria quietly went with her.

Jack looked at Zane. "I've got a problem." He explained what had happened. When he finished, he shook his head. "I didn't expect this complication, and I'm running out of options. Rita's going to see if the nanny service has someone for emergency service."

"If they don't?"

"I don't know."

Zane frowned. "If the nanny service doesn't pan out, there's the center on the ground level. I know they'll take her and she'll be safe. Great people."

He'd been avoiding that idea, just for the simple reason he didn't want Victoria in a crowd of strange kids. For some reason, that worried him, and he wasn't sure why. She'd been brought all this way to be with a man who was little more than a stranger. How could he put her in a place where she'd be surrounded by strange faces? "I'll see what Rita comes up with, and if she strikes out, I might have to take you up on it."

"We'll only be another half hour, then we can break for lunch. That should give you time to do what you need to do before the afternoon conference with Sommers…if he hooks on with us."

Feeling disoriented and frustrated, Jack went back into the room with Zane. He hadn't expected things to be easy with Victoria, but he hadn't expected them to be such a struggle, either. Rita had mentioned a neighbor watching Victoria, and all he could think of was Rain with the child, Rain giving the child a massage and feeding her horrible tea. He almost smiled at that image, until he looked up and saw the screen by the table. They hadn't had to wait until afternoon to have E. J. Sommers join them on a hookup from New York.

Jack sank down in his chair and looked at the man who seemed more at home on a ranch than in a board room. He wasn't smiling as Zane greeted him. He looked angry.

JACK CALLED RITA as soon as he could get out of the tense meeting, and received the bad news that there was nothing that could be done in the way of child care for today. So, he headed down to the center, promising Rita he'd get back to her within fifteen minutes.

When he actually saw the center, it wasn't at all what Jack expected. It seemed to be a happy place, with happy kids, and noise vibrating off the walls that were covered with murals of children doing exactly what they were doing in the center. Playing. The older woman, who had been showing him around and had introduced herself simply as Mary, was happy, too. He was glad it was such an upbeat situation. Victoria really needed happiness in her life, and he needed to get back to work.

He quickly explained about Victoria's situation and his predicament, and the smile on the older woman's face faded a bit.

"Oh, I am so very sorry for both of you," she said, and touched his arm. "You poor things."

Her sympathy was as disconcerting as her smiles had been moments ago. He'd never thought of himself as a "poor thing." "Thank you," he said politely.

Then the smile was back full force. "We would love to have your child come and join us. We're open from seven in the morning until seven at night. Parents and guardians are all welcome to visit any time. In fact, we encourage adult involvement on every level and the children adore it, too."

"I just need her to be cared for today and maybe tomorrow."

''Whatever you need, we're here,'' she said. ''Just a few things I should know.''

He glanced at his watch. ''Okay.''

''What does the child want to be called?''

''Victoria, I suppose. She doesn't speak.''

She frowned. ''She's mute?''

''No, not at all. She can hear and speak, but right now she's choosing not to talk.''

This really made the woman look beyond concerned, then her expression cleared slightly. ''You know, I've always believed that everything works out the way it should. I mean, it's been just awful for you with the nanny leaving, and you having to bring the little girl here all the way from London, then not being able to get the new nanny for a couple of days. And this whole business thing going on. But, you know, it could be for the best, no matter how dark it looks at the moment.''

He didn't need a rundown on what his life was like or a pep talk from a woman who seemed to be an eternal optimist. ''How is this for the good?'' he asked, his patience wearing a bit thin.

''You came in here with a child who is obviously troubled, and the very same day, we have a clinical psychologist starting whose specialty is children. From what I've seen, she's wonderful, she has that special rapport with the little people that we all wish we had. Best of all, she's here on staff. What would you think of her talking to Victoria, maybe just check her out a bit and try to find out what the child is thinking or worrying about?''

He'd give anything to know what was going on behind those eyes. And he'd thought about getting professional help once they got back to London. Mary might be right. This could be a good thing in the midst of the chaos. "What's her background?"

"She's fully licensed to practice, had only glowing recommendations, and she's associated with the Children's Hospital, the very one we're having the charity ball for to raise funds for their new wing. A lovely, caring woman."

"Okay, I'd be willing to pay whatever it costs."

"Oh, no, it's all part of what the center offers. We just want to help the little ones." Then she grinned at him. "But, you could make a nice donation to the charity ball fund."

"Absolutely," he said.

"Wonderful." She clasped her hands together, then she looked past him and the smile was gone suddenly and completely.

He followed her line of vision and saw Robert coming into the center through the main entrance. He stopped, saw Jack, then came over to him. "Is everything under control?"

"I think so," he said as he turned to Mary, but she was gone. He looked around at the area by the huge play tree, but she was nowhere in sight. Then Brittany was hurrying over to her father, her flame-colored hair was free and wild, and paint spotted her jeans and shirt. She gave Robert a huge hug, then looked at Jack, "So, did Mary talk you into bringing the little girl down for a while?"

"As a matter of fact, she did."

"Who would have thought, you with a child?" she asked with a grin. "Life does have its little surprises.'' Before he could say anything, she turned to her father. ''Did you come to get Jack?''

''I came to see if Anthony was coming home with me this afternoon?''

''He sure is and thrilled about your new train. As soon as he gets here from school, I'll run him up to you.''

''Great.'' He looked at Jack. ''My grandson, Anthony. He's almost ten, and he's a man after my own heart about trains.''

Jack had assumed the child was an infant. ''Who would have thought of you with a child?'' he said to Brittany.

''Yeah, who would have?'' she said. ''And he's a great kid. We're lucky to have him.'' She looked back at Robert. ''Since you're here, could you take a look at the court papers we received today?''

Robert glanced at his watch, then nodded. ''Can we do it in ten minutes?''

''We will do it in nine,'' she said, hooking her arm in her father's and taking him over to the center's kitchen.

''See you upstairs,'' Robert called over his shoulder, then went into the kitchen with Brittany.

The door swung shut behind the two of them, and Jack turned to see Mary coming toward him from the back area. ''Sorry, an emergency,'' she said, although he hadn't seen or heard a thing. ''Are you going to bring Victoria down now?''

He nodded. ''I'll go and get her, then—''

''Talk about things working out,'' Mary said, looking past Jack as her smile grew. ''Here's the doctor now. You two can talk a bit before the child is around.''

That would make life simpler Jack thought as he turned, but the moment he saw the doctor, life just got more and more complicated. Rain. Rain, in faded jeans, a T-shirt with a logo of a sixties band on it, and her long hair tamed in a single braid that skimmed it off of her makeup free face. Rain who said she didn't work here and never once mentioned being a doctor. A child therapist? No. There had to be someone behind her, someone Mary was talking to, but there wasn't anyone except kids between Rain and the entry door.

Then any illusion he'd had that there'd been a mistake, vanished when Mary said, ''Rain, how lovely and what good timing. I was just talking to Mr. Ford about you.'' Then she cemented it with, ''Mr. Ford, this is our doctor.''

''Doctor?'' he repeated, and he hated the way she was almost smiling now, as if she could read his disbelief and discomfort and was enjoying it. She seemed to know how he was reacting to her before he did himself.

''Dr. Rainbow Swan Armstrong,'' she murmured. ''And why does Mary think we need to talk?''

''We don't,'' Jack said abruptly.

''Oh, but my yes,'' Mary said right away. ''Of course you do.'' She moved closer to Rain. ''Mr. Ford has a little girl who might need a bit of help. She's had great loss in her life, and she's sort of shut down. She doesn't speak at all.''

He at least had the satisfaction of seeing surprise on Rain's face when Mary mentioned Victoria. But she covered it neatly with concern before it was too obvious. "A little girl?" Rain asked the woman, but looked at Jack.

"A four-year-old child named Victoria. She's upstairs at the moment. And she needs help." She turned to Jack. "Wouldn't you say that about sums it up?"

"Yes, of course, but—"

Mary cut him off when she touched his arm, and said with great concern, "I have an idea. Why don't you both go up to get Victoria, let the doctor and child meet, then Rain can bring Victoria back down here? You do have an important meeting starting soon, don't you?"

He was backed neatly into a corner, both by circumstances and by Mary. But Rain gave him an out. "Mary, that's a lovely idea, but I think Mr. Ford would like some time to think this over. I'm not…well, maybe I'm not quite what he was thinking of to help his little girl."

It was a perfect out. But before he had a chance, Mary destroyed it with logic. "Nonsense. He needs help and you have the time to give it. What's not good about that?"

"Yes, what's not good about that?" Rain asked as she looked right at Jack.

He knew she was counting on him to say something about her in front of Mary. He thought she'd like that in some way, maybe to prove her point about him, that he was uptight and judgmental. But he wasn't going to say what he wanted to say right now in front of Mary. "I guess we could talk in the elevator," he said.

She seemed taken aback that he even agreed to talk to her. "We could talk here," she countered.

He shook his head. "Don't have time. I need to get upstairs, so you'll have to come along with me to talk."

She handed Mary her bag and said, "Could you put that in the office for me? I'll be back soon."

"Perfect," the older lady said with a smile. "Go, talk and get to know each other." She looked slightly flustered for a moment, then said, "You need to discuss the child."

Jack and Rain left in silence. It wasn't until Jack pushed the elevator call button that Rain finally spoke. "Okay, just say whatever you're dying to say and get it over with before you explode."

He looked at her and she was staring at the closed elevator doors, not at him. "You're such a liar," he muttered.

That made her look at him with wide eyes and gasp, "What?"

The doors to the elevator slid open and he stepped inside, then turned and motioned her into the car with him. He didn't want to do this in public. He held the door with his left hand to keep it open. "Get in," he said.

She hesitated, and for a moment he thought she was going to turn and walk away. He didn't want her to do that. He wanted to say what he wanted to say, then she could leave in a huff if she wanted to. "Get in," he said again.

She glared at him, her cheeks flushed, but she silently stepped into the car and he let go of the doors. "I am not a liar," she said tightly as the doors slid shut.

"Could have fooled me," he murmured as he jabbed the button for the top floor with more force than he intended. "You said you didn't work here, and you do. You never said you were a doctor and apparently you are."

"First, I don't work here, I volunteer. And secondly, you never asked if I was a doctor and I never said I wasn't. But, I see what this is all about," she said, glaring at him now.

"I'm sure you're going to tell me, aren't you?"

Her rich brown eyes narrowed on him. "You're thinking, 'She's a doctor? A doctor of what? Meditation?' Or maybe you're thinking, 'Where did she do her training, at a commune?' Or the clincher, 'I wouldn't let her examine a turnip.'"

"Don't make this about me," he said, the car lurching slightly before it continued up silently. "It's about you and the things you conveniently forgot to tell me."

Rain had always tried to be open and honest. If she wasn't, she would have let him think she was in some crazy live-in relationship and it would have put up a barrier between the two of them. A safe barrier. "Well, you sure omitted a few things yourself, like that you have a daughter."

"You never asked."

"You never said. So we're even."

"I don't think so."

"You're not going to let me talk to your daughter,

are you?'' she asked, and felt unsettled that it upset her. The one thing she did and did well was to help troubled children. And it sounded like this one really needed her help.

Chapter Six

Rain watched Jack carefully as he shrugged. "Why should I?"

"I'm very good at what I do," she countered.

He looked at her. "Where did you get your credentials?"

He never stopped. "A commune," she said.

He actually smiled slightly. "Ah, you're trying to see if I have a sense of humor yet, aren't you?"

"No." She couldn't smile. "Sorry. I was home schooled, got my high school diploma at sixteen, went right into college, found out what I wanted to do, clinical psychology, and followed it right through to a Ph.D., specializing in childhood therapy. My degree is from Berkeley, and I'm licensed to work in this state. I'll be on staff at the Children's Hospital in a few weeks, but until then, I'm volunteering here. And, best of all, although I know you must be filthy rich, I'm free. No charge. No out-of-pocket expenses for my services."

His expression tightened as she spoke. He definitely was not impressed; and the thing was, she never tried to impress anyone. But something in her wanted him to say, "Well, you're qualified," at least. Instead, he said, "That doesn't matter," as the car slid to a stop with a soft chime.

She stayed where she was, waiting for him to walk away and never look back. "Is this where you say, 'Thanks, but no thanks'?"

"This is where I ask if you're coming?"

She was surprised, but moved quickly out of the elevator. He stopped once they reached the corridor, his gaze studying her intently, making her feel incredibly uncomfortable. Finally she blurted out, "Look, I'm a real doctor, a real therapist. I don't do witch doctoring and I don't use magic herbs or say chants under a full moon."

She expected him to get angry again, but he didn't. "Why are you a doctor?" he asked as if he really wanted to know.

"Why are you what you are?" she countered.

He hesitated, then said, "That's a long story."

"Well, my story isn't. Kids have always fascinated me. They hurt more deeply than adults because they don't understand all of the reasons or ramifications in life. And they need someone who can help, or at least try to help."

"Do you have any children?" The question took her slightly off guard.

She'd thought about children from time to time, but even though she loved her parents, she knew that having her had been hard on them. She truly felt that her well-being was what drove her mother to leave her father and go "traditional." "I'm doing this for you, Rain, so you can have more stability in your life," she been told more than once, and also heard the unsaid words in that statement. "If it wasn't for you, I'd be doing something totally different with my life and doing it with Dune." She wouldn't do that to a child, and her life was never going to be traditional.

"No. Do you have any more children?" she asked. "Any little Jack Fords running around making huge business deals and wearing three-piece suits?"

What she'd intended as a tension breaker, only seemed to deepen it. "No," he said. "And Victoria isn't my child. She's my ward. I'm her guardian. Her father was my best friend, all the way from college, through our first law firm, and when he and his wife were pregnant with Victoria, they asked me to be her godfather and to look after her if they couldn't." She saw the way his jaw tensed, and the way he rocked slowly forward on the balls of his feet. "I never thought I'd have to do it, but..." He shrugged. "Life has its surprises."

She could feel the pain in him and knew that if she told him she admired him for taking the child on, he wouldn't want that. "Her parents?"

"They came to London from Los Angeles about six months ago, with Victoria in tow. Ian had a job assignment there for a year. They were out, in the rain, and another car ran a signal. The next thing I knew, they were gone, and Victoria was mine."

She ached for both of them. "It's hard to take care of a child alone," was all she said.

"Eve and I are getting married next year, maybe sooner, and then there'll be a home for her, something solid and secure."

She didn't ask where Eve was, why she wasn't here building a bond with the child. It wasn't her business, no more than it was her business to feel a strange ache in her middle at the thought of their happy family. She'd never craved that as a child, but at that moment, it struck a chord in her. "Well, I think you've got everything set."

Jack shrugged, then started walking, and she fell in step beside him. "I'm trying, but Victoria doesn't talk. She just does what she's told to do. She was with a nanny and that fell through, so I thought bringing her here would be a good idea, instead of letting Eve hire another nanny for her. Another stranger to care for her."

Eve obviously wasn't going to care for her, and that raised a bit of anger in Rain. "You did the right thing."

He didn't look as if he believed her, but he didn't argue. "I did what I had to do."

She knew that single sentence defined the man. He was a person who was intensely responsible. A fixer. A man who took up pieces and tried to make them whole. No wonder men like George rankled him. Men whom he perceived as being irresponsible. And people like her, folded into the same perception. She understood more about Jack Ford in that moment than ever before, and she had a clearer picture of why he did what he did.

"Victoria's an American, although she traveled all over the world with Ian and Jean, so this wasn't a huge cultural shock for her coming to Houston. But I don't have any way to take care of her and do business, too. That's why I went to the center until the nanny we've found can take over in a few days."

"You're going to keep her at the loft with you?"

He stopped by Zane Holden's office. Jack didn't open the door, but turned to Rain. "For now. I really can't move. Besides, I'll only be here for another week or two, tops." She must have frowned, because he asked, "Is there a problem with the loft?"

"It's not safe for a child, I wouldn't think."

"Why?"

"It's on the second floor and there's outside access to the fire escape." She felt slight heat in her cheeks at the memory of the last time she'd been on the fire escape and what had happened. But she kept talking, trying to ignore the images that came to her. "Even if Victoria is lethargic and quiet, she could still get out on to it, and…" She shrugged. "It could be dangerous."

He nodded. "I'll lock it."

"Good idea," she said.

"Anything else?"

"Does she have a pacifier?"

He shook his head. "A pacifier? She's four years old."

"Sorry, I didn't mean that literally. I meant a toy, a blanket, something that she uses for comfort."

"Oh, a doll. She keeps it with her all the time."

"Does the doll have a name?"

"Probably, but since she isn't talking, I don't know what it is." He reached for the door handle then, but this time she stopped him.

"No, wait a minute."

He looked down at her. "What?"

She wanted to help these two people, even without meeting the little girl, but she had to ask him one thing. "Are you sure you want me to do this?"

Jack hesitated before answering, and that bothered Rain. When he spoke, it bothered her even more. "She has to be at the center today and maybe tomorrow, and since you're there, I don't think it would hurt."

That was hardly a statement that showed he had even an iota of faith in her, and she reacted in a way she shouldn't have to his words. Emotionally. It hurt. She wanted him to see her for what she was, someone who wanted to help and had the training to do so. Not as a passing convenience that he'd use despite his feelings about her personally. But since the first moment she'd seen him in the kitchen, her reactions to him had all been based on emotion. Fear at the very first, then a whole range of emotions. But always that intense awareness of him when he was near. This wasn't a game. A child's well-being was at stake and she hesitated.

He frowned at her. "Do you want to do it?"

She wasn't going to lie. "Yes, very much so."

He pushed open the door and held it back for her to go in ahead of him. She went past him, and saw a familiar face first, Rita, the lady from the elevator, sitting behind the reception desk. Then she saw the child. The minute she met the gaze from those blue eyes, she knew she'd done the right thing. Whatever she felt about Jack or his motives, the child was there, hugging a pitiful rag doll. She needed help.

Victoria sat in a blue fabric armchair, her little feet in black patent leather shoes that dangled above the low-nap carpeting. She was a tiny thing, in a navy dress that was fussy and stiff-looking, worn with white tights. She had that aura of fragility that Rain had seen so many times in children going through a traumatic experience. Her pale-blond hair was caught back severely in twin braids, only emphasizing her pallid skin and overly large eyes.

She stared at Rain for a moment, glanced at Jack, then down at the doll. There was no emotion in her expression, and no response to either herself or Jack. Rain thought that the child's avoidance of speech was probably the least of their worries. Jack had his hands full, and a part of her admired him for sticking with this and trying to make it work. A lot of people would walk away from a child like this, pawn her off on the system, but Jack wasn't doing that.

Rita was speaking to Jack, but Rain was focused on the child. She moved to where she sat, and crouched down in front of her. "Victoria? I'm Rain. I came all the way up here to meet you because I've heard so many wonderful things about you." The child wasn't buying it and didn't even look at Rain. But she kept on. "I was wondering if you'd like to come downstairs with me? There's a terrific place down there where kids play and have fun and just get goofy and we'd all love it if you'd come down and share it with us."

Victoria shifted slightly, but never took her eyes off her doll. Rain could feel that a part of the child wanted desperately to play and not be so sad, but she didn't know how anymore. Rain had seen it so many times in these situations.

"Would you like to play?" Rain asked again.

"She's been fine," she heard Rita saying behind her. "Oh, a bit too quiet, but very good."

Rain knew Victoria was listening. She bet the child

heard everything. She hoped that they were careful
what they said in front of her. So much pain was only
multiplied for children when they were treated as if
they were invisible, as if they couldn't hear or see. It
wasn't intentional, but it was damaging.

JACK WAS WATCHING Rain and Victoria, but listening
to Rita. ''Bad news from the nanny agency,'' she
said.

Jack frowned, not wanting any bad news at the moment. ''What now?'' he asked.

''They had that nanny, but she can't do it, but
there's a Mrs. Williams, who comes with very high
references, and she can start in three days. But, she'll
work on a temp basis, and on a sleep-out basis. I
thought that might work with the lack of space at the
loft. I hope that's acceptable.''

Picturing the three days looming in front of him,
he asked, ''Isn't there any way to get her to start
sooner?''

''No, that's the best they can do.''

He watched Rain gently touch the matted orange
wool hair of the rag doll, and Victoria didn't move.
''I've arranged for her to go the center for the rest of
the day, and we can do it for a few more days.'' Rain
drew back, but stayed close to the child, talking in a
soft voice that Jack couldn't make out. ''I'll have to
wing it at the loft for a while, I guess.''

He saw the way Rain got to the child's level and
stayed there, patiently. Waiting. But not touching her
or pushing her into anything. She was just there. No
matter what his misgivings had been, he found himself glad that she'd come in here with him.

"Did Avery get the loft fixed for you?" Rita was asking.

Avery? He didn't recognize the name for a moment, then remembered the lady whom Rita had sent to the loft to set up the bed and fill the refrigerator with a wide assortment of food. "Yes, she got it fixed just fine. Now, I need to get—"

The ring of his cell phone interrupted him and he took it out to answer it. "Ford here."

"Where is here?" Zane asked.

"Your office. Where're you?"

"Ready to start the meeting. Sommers can only give us another half hour or so."

Damn Sommers. He wasn't a businessman. He'd lucked into the whole conglomerate thing by being able to improve on any given object or any system in place. But he was making them jump through hoops, blaming them for the bombardment of takeover threats he was experiencing since the leak of their negotiations hit the business world. "I'll be there as soon as I can get there," he muttered and closed his cell phone.

"I need to get to that meeting," he said to Rain. "Do you think you can take care of getting her down to the center and everything?"

She turned without standing and looked up at Jack. "I suppose so, but I think you need to explain to Victoria what we're going to do."

That made sense. He went closer to the two of them, and stood behind Rain, looking down at the child. "Rain is going to take you down to play while I work, then we'll go back to the loft where we're going to live for a while." The little girl finally responded by looking up at him, her expression bleak. He knew something was bothering her, but he had no option but to guess at the cause. He looked at his watch. Almost one in the afternoon. It was well into evening in London. Jet lag? "You're probably confused and tired."

The expression only intensified.

"Okay, you don't want to play?"

She stayed still, never taking her eyes off of him.

He glanced at Rain. "Any ideas?"

She didn't answer him, but spoke right to Victoria. "Maybe you'd like to stay with…" She looked at Jack again. "What does she call you?"

"Uncle Jack."

"Maybe you'd like to stay with Uncle Jack?"

He was shocked when Victoria moved quickly, scooting off the chair and getting as close as she could to his right side without actually touching him. Rain did read minds, he thought with a sinking feeling. "That's out of the question. The meeting's ready to start and it's no place for her."

Rain stood. "Well…?" She looked past him at Rita. "Is there a place near the conference room where we could sit for a while?"

"A side room with chairs and a television they use for presentations when they need to."

"Great." She looked back at Jack. "What if I stay with Victoria by your conference room and get some toys up from the center? Maybe that'll help her transition."

It made sense to him. "Sure," he said and frowned when his cell phone rang again.

He flipped it open. "Yes?"

"He's online," Zane said, and didn't have to say who was online. Jack knew.

"I'm on my way," he said, closed the phone, then looked at Victoria. "Victoria, I have to go to work, but if you'd like, Rain can stay with you by the room until I can get out. Do you think that would be okay?"

The little girl looked up at him, and for the first time, she actually responded. It was slight, but definite. The suggestion of a nod that he would have missed if he hadn't been so desperate for any response at all.

"Great," he said, and looked at Rain. "Let's get going."

Jack went with Victoria out into the corridor and headed for the conference room. He knew Rain was following them, but she held back. When they got to the conference room, he pushed back the door and went in, spotted the room to the left with several chairs, a couch, some low tables and a wall mounted television.

He stopped and looked down at Victoria. He could hear raised voices coming through the partially open door of the conference room. "Stay with Rain, Victoria, and I'll be right in there." He pointed to the door. "I'll be out as soon as I can get this done. Okay?"

The child didn't respond, not even the suggestion of a nod, but she didn't look panicked, either. He looked at Rain who had come to stand behind Victoria. "I don't know how long I'll be."

"Don't worry. We'll be fine. If we aren't here when you come out, we'll be downstairs."

He felt at least part of his burden lighten, and he simply said, ''Thank you,'' then headed into the conference room.

JACK CAME OUT of the meeting four hours later, drained and frustrated. All of them were. Sommers wasn't an easy man to deal with, and Jack had finally figured out why. It wasn't the money. The man had millions, maybe billions. He just plain didn't like being manipulated, and he felt that was exactly what was happening. The leak, the section of his corporation on the chopping block. The possibility of a hostile takeover. LynTech had to repair the damage and make Sommers come into their camp.

Games. God, he hated them. He'd hated them for as long as he could remember, starting with the way his father did things. He'd been in the business long enough to know that morality didn't always play a key role in actions or decision making, and game playing only underscored it, the way his father's actions had underscored it.

Robert was beside him as he left. He was a moral man. He'd run this business with an underlying principle of fairness, but toughness. He'd made things work and work well. ''What do you think, Robert?'' Jack asked as they stepped out of the conference room.

The older man looked drained as he shook his head. ''I think this is a world where I don't fit anymore.''

''No, that's not true. You fit, and you're needed. We just have to get back on track with Sommers.''

Robert smiled slightly. ''Exactly. Right now I'm hungry. I'm going out with Brittany, Matt and Anthony. Would you like to come along and take a breather?''

''Thanks, but I've got things to do.''

''I hope it's not work,'' Robert said.

Jack glanced at the older man. ''Not entirely, but I've got to contact Japan again.''

Robert shook his head. ''Jack, you know, you're not Clayton. You don't have to prove that you aren't, not to me.''

Any mention of his father was not welcome. ''I'm not doing that.''

''Aren't you? Isn't that why you came on board ten years ago? Some sort of atonement for what you thought your father did to me and this company?''

Robert had never mentioned anything like this before and it stunned Jack. Atonement. Hell, yes it was atonement. And he doubted that he could ever make up for what damage his father had done to everyone—Robert, his mother, so many others. ''Robert, I'm just trying to do what needs to be done. Don't make it some sort of martyrdom on my part.''

Robert frowned, then patted Jack on the shoulder. ''I just want you to know that I want you here, that I've always wanted you here, and not to make up for Clayton on any level.'' He smiled slightly then. ''And I'm thrilled that you're getting married. You need someone to be there with you. And to Damon Ryder's daughter. She and Brittany used to do a lot together. She's a lovely woman.''

''She's great.''

''You love her?''

Love? His idea of love wasn't his mother's blind adoration of Clayton Ford, even when the man was irresponsible and causing untold damage. Love was deciding that you wanted to spend your life with someone and knowing why. He was marrying Eve, and that said it all. "Of course I love her."

"When's the big day?"

"We haven't been able to pin it down yet. There's a lot to do, and I have a few personal things I need to get in line."

His smile faltered. "Oh, my yes, I heard about that little child you took in. What a sad thing for her...and for you."

Victoria. He'd blocked out everything during the afternoon meeting, and now he turned and looked into the side room. It was empty. They were probably down at the center. "It's been difficult, but we'll make it work," he said.

"Of course," Robert said. "And if I can help you in any way, just ask, okay?"

"Absolutely."

"Good, good," Robert said, then called to Matt who was just stepping out of the conference room, "Matthew?"

Jack watched the two men leave and would have gone out and down to the center, but something in the side room caught his eye. On a low table, he saw papers, but they weren't business papers. They were crayon drawings. He went closer and found out the room wasn't empty at all. Tucked off to the right on a low couch, he saw Rain and Victoria. They were both asleep.

Victoria was low on the cushions, hugging the doll to her middle, her head to one side, almost resting on her own shoulder, and her tiny feet in the white tights, the shoes gone, resting on the low table close to the front of the couch. Rain was right next to her, her head against the couch back, her feet resting on the table beside Victoria's, and bare. Her hands were at her sides, her right hand barely touching the foot of the old doll. Her lashes lay darkly against her cheeks in arcs, and she breathed very slowly.

He moved closer, and realized that Victoria actually looked peaceful. Relaxed. Something he hadn't seen since the day she'd been brought to his house.

He moved to the edge of the table and looked down at the pictures. He saw stick people in dark colors, in a row, hands at their sides and blank circles for eyes. There were scrawls that might have been trees or flowers, but he wasn't sure. What he recognized was the rain, huge drops in dark blue scribbled all over the papers. A sad picture, and he didn't have to ask what it meant.

He put his briefcase on the table and reached down to touch Rain's bare toes to get her attention, but he stopped in midmotion when her eyes opened and met her brown gaze. She shifted carefully, lifting her hand to touch her lips with her forefinger to hush him, then slid off the couch and came around the table to get closer to him.

The top of her head barely came to his shoulders, and she had to tip her head back to look up at him. "I almost gave up on you ever coming out of there," she said in a whisper.

"It took longer than I imagined," he said, matching her tone. "She wouldn't go downstairs?"

"We've been downstairs, and she ate and saw the other children. But it was getting late and she had had enough. So, I brought her up here to wait for you to get out.''

''What went on?''

She glanced at the sleeping child. ''A lot. But all good, I think,'' she whispered, meeting his gaze again from under those long lashes. ''She isn't talking, but once I assured her I was a friend, and that I lived next to the loft, that we were going to be neighbors for a while, she eased up a bit. She drew a few things and watched the other kids play.'' She shrugged. ''I think she just wants to be connected again, to find what she lost. She needs that desperately. I know it's impossible for her to get back what she's lost, but she needs something else to take its place. She really needs bonding.''

Jack knew it was all true, so very true, and he nodded. ''I wish I knew how to do that,'' he said with aching honesty.

Rain glanced at Victoria again, and then said what she'd been thinking since she'd met the little girl. ''If you want my professional opinion, I think it's vital that she bonds with you and with your fiancée. I think it's a good idea to give her stability and family.''

Rain felt passionately about what she told Jack, and it was jarring to her when he said, ''Well, I didn't expect to get that sort of advice from you.''

She'd heard bits and pieces of him talking to the other man a few minutes earlier, and caught the tension in his voice when he spoke about his father. She'd also heard him say he loved Eve, but something in his tone wasn't right. And it wasn't right now. ''Why not?'' she asked in a whisper, knowing she was going to regret asking even before he answered her.

"You're endorsing family stability."

She felt heat in her cheeks, and hated the way he could make her blush like that. "I'm not the issue here, Victoria is, and that's what she needs. That and a lot of love. It's up to you and your fiancée to give her what she needs, not me. I'm just giving you my professional opinion. You're free to take it or leave it." She almost said she didn't care what he did with it, but the fact of the matter was, she cared, very much.

In truth, both the man and child made her care, and for totally different reasons. And because she cared, she'd tried to help Jack relax at her loft. A mistake then, and a mistake now. It was time for her to leave, for her own sake as much as for any other reason.

Chapter Seven

Rain turned from Jack, looked around blindly, then went to the edge of the couch to get her shoes. She stepped into them, then turned, trying to contain her anger. It was hard enough being with the child for so long, trying to get into her head and figure out the horrors that were hiding in there. And when she'd managed to get her to trust her a bit, when she'd managed to get her to take a nap, she'd felt a victory of sorts. Until she'd heard the voices in the outer room.

She'd intended to get up then, to meet Jack before he came into the room, but she hadn't. Instead, she'd eavesdropped, and tried to figure out another piece of the puzzle called Jackson Ford. From his tone, he had old issues with his father. That wasn't all that uncommon in adults. Although she'd never truly understood it. She'd never wanted to be like George, but if someone had told her she was like him in some way, she'd be pleased.

Now all she wanted to do was to walk out the door and not look back. She wasn't comfortable being this close to Jack. She didn't want his criticism or his sarcasm. She needed air. But she couldn't just leave with Victoria still asleep. She'd promised her she'd be there when she woke. She would be. No matter what. But she wasn't going to give Jack free reign to put her down whenever he wanted to.

"You know, I don't understand what you have against me," she said getting closer and whispering. She narrowed her eyes. "I know you think I'm different, that my father's different. Heck, you haven't even met my mother, but I can assure you, she's very different."

He was so controlled, so able to hide anger or shock. He simply said in a half whisper, "I wasn't talking about your father, or about your mother."

"No, you were talking about me," she said, hating that she was unable to let this go.

She saw his jaw work, then amazingly, he was apologizing. "I'm sorry. I'm tired, and frustrated."

Any anger was gone when she finally saw the heaviness in the man, the way the lines at his eyes and mouth seemed deeper now than they had just a few hours ago. "Things didn't go well in there?"

"Not even close," he said and looked at the child. "How long do you think she'll sleep?"

As if on cue, Victoria stirred, and her eyes fluttered open. For a moment Rain saw disorientation in her eyes, touched by fear. Rain moved quickly around the table and crouched by the child. "Sweetheart, it's okay. Uncle Jack's here." She motioned behind her. "I promised he'd come back and he did."

The child looked at the man and her tension seemed to ease. "Did you have a good nap?" Rain asked.

Victoria looked at her, then rubbed her eyes with one hand, and yawned. "Good, good," Rain said in a soothing voice, then moved back a bit and nodded in Jack's direction. "Uncle Jack came to take you to the loft we talked about, the place you're going to live for a while and you get to meet Joey, the cat."

"Why don't you get your shoes, Victoria, and we can get going?" Jack said.

Victoria hesitated, then slid off and bent down to reach under the table. A moment later she stood with the shoes in one hand, her doll still in the other. She looked at Jack, then at Rain, and Rain took the child's shoes from her. "Sit down, sweetie, and I'll put them back on you," she said and Victoria allowed it.

Done, Rain gave her a small hug, and stood. "I'll see you tomorrow, sweetie, I promise. Remember, I told you I'd be here when you came to the center downstairs? I'll be waiting for you right by the door."

Rain could tell that Victoria didn't want to go but didn't have the heart to fight anything. The child simply went over to where Jack stood, ready to do whatever he asked of her. He touched her on the top of her head. "Ready?"

She glanced at Rain, then up at Jack. Even Rain couldn't read her expression. There simply wasn't any except resignation. "Tomorrow at the center?" Rain said.

Jack looked at her over Victoria. "Tomorrow at the center," he said and the man and child left.

Rain stood there for a long moment, totally unprepared for the sense of aloneness she experienced once they were out of the area. Or for the feeling that she should have gone with them, that she should have helped get Victoria settled in the loft. That was ridiculous. Not needed. Jack was there, and despite everything, she knew that he'd do whatever was needed.

She left the conference room, stepped out into the corridor and headed for the elevators. As she pushed the call button, she heard someone coming down the hallway and looked up to see Rita hurrying toward the elevators. "Hi, there," she said. "How did it work out with Victoria?"

"Okay," she murmured as the doors opened with a soft chime and the two women got into the car. Rita pushed the lobby button and Rain leaned back against the coolness of the elevator wall. "She's so sweet."

Rita smiled. "Just a doll. I've got two boys and I've always wanted a little girl."

"Did you meet Mr. Ford's fiancée at the airport?"

Rita frowned. "Yes, I did."

"What is she like?" Rain heard herself ask.

"Honestly?"

"Just between you and me."

"Okay, I didn't like her. You would have thought she was passing off a piece of luggage when she gave me Victoria. All she could think about was getting her connecting flight. She was babbling about some villa and some people with little dogs. I had a feeling she was glad to be rid of the child." She bit her lip. "Sorry, I shouldn't have said that. It's really not my place, none of my business."

No it wasn't, and it wasn't any of Rain's business, either. But that didn't stop a slight sickness in her middle or a sense of anger at a woman she didn't even know. "She went from here to Mexico?"

"Acapulco, apparently. She said something about

the villa and friends who would just be crushed if she was late.'' She grimaced. ''I hate to see people get crushed, don't you?''

Rain smiled. ''Oh, yes, a horrible thing to happen.''

The elevator stopped and as they stepped out, she and Rita both crossed to the center. ''My boys are waiting,'' Rita said, and went inside with Rain.

Rita headed for the kitchen when someone told her that her sons were helping a worker clean up after a cookie baking spree, and Rain went back to the office to get her bag and leave. She stepped inside and Mary was there, sitting behind the desk. The woman looked slightly pale. Rain crossed to the desk. ''Mary, are you all right?''

The older woman looked up and dots of high color touched her cheeks. She exhaled in a rush. ''Fine, fine,'' she murmured. ''You were gone so long, I thought you'd already left for the day.''

''No, I needed to stay with Victoria. I've come to get my bag.'' She hesitated. ''Are you sure things are okay? You look as though you've seen a ghost.''

Mary exhaled and shook her head briskly, then sat up straighter. ''Ghosts? Oh, my, we all have them in our past, don't we?'' she said, then stood as she gathered up papers. ''Will you be in tomorrow?''

''Yes, I'll be in first thing in the morning. I promised Victoria I'd be here when she arrived.''

Mary fiddled with the papers. ''They're a sad pair, aren't they?''

''They've both had a great loss, his friends and her parents.''

Mary looked right at Rain. ''What do you think of our Mr. Ford?''

Our Mr. Ford? "What do I think of him?"

"Yes, your impressions, your opinions?"

"Well, he's fine. He's taking care of the little girl. He's a hard worker."

"He's very attractive, don't you think?" she asked.

She stared at Mary, at those soft eyes that apparently saw more then she thought they did. "He's engaged."

"He's not married, not yet."

"He's getting married, but he's…stuffy, and conservative, and so tense, he's like a coiled spring all the time."

Mary came around the desk, patted Rain on the arm, then said, "Teach him how to relax, dear," then walked out of the office leaving Rain to stare after her in amazement.

JACK MANAGED TO GET HOME with Victoria, to make her a peanut-butter-and-jelly sandwich with milk, and get her into her nightgown. At least the child was obedient and didn't fight him. When he put her into bed, she settled down under the covers, and when he told her good-night, she closed her eyes. He didn't know when she really went to sleep, but she was asleep when he looked in on her an hour later.

He worked in peace until midnight, amazed that it was that easy. Put her to bed, then work. He was relieved, then he heard something outside, a rattling sound, and the cat dived in through an open upper window. He landed with great skill on the workstation desk, barely missing the fax machine, then made his way with considerable agility through the maze of cables and stacked papers to get right up to Jack's computer screen.

He mewed plaintively at Jack. He'd totally forgotten about the cat. He stood, went into the kitchen, put some cat food in the dish, then set it on the floor. ''If you want it, get it and if you don't, don't,'' he said, going back to the computer.

The cat sat there for a very long moment, then finally jumped off the table onto the floor and went over to the food. Jack sat back in the chair, but glanced up at the open louvers in the hinged window near the ceiling when he heard another noise outside. Lutes? Or something exotic sounding. Music that was more sound than melody. He got up, went to the fire escape window, opened it, making a mental note to find out about a child proof lock, then glanced out.

Rain was there, on the other fire escape landing, sitting as she had before, cross-legged, face lifted to the night sky. The music was coming from her loft. He watched her until she shifted, brought her head down, then up again, her hair loose and falling around her shoulders and down her back. He moved back, closed the window quietly, and found himself taking several deep breaths, as if getting more air into his lungs could stop the response he felt deep inside. He exhaled again, raked his fingers through his hair, then went back to the desk. He sat down, stared at the screen in front of him, then reached for the phone.

He dialed the number in Acapulco that Eve had left for him. They needed to talk. He needed to make sure she'd gotten in okay. He needed... He closed his eyes when a machine picked up on the other end. A voice he didn't recognize asked him to please leave a message, but he didn't and hung up. "Damn it," he muttered and went back to work.

RAIN WAS AT THE CENTER at eight in the morning, and helped put out the painting supplies, then made sandwiches with Brittany and her son, Anthony, for the group of children going on a planned outing. Anthony pushed the last sandwich into its plastic wrapper, then looked at Brittany. "I gotta go. The van's ready." He smiled at Rain. "Nice to meet ya, ma'am. You're a good sandwich maker."

The child was a smooth talker, quite a guy, with curly dark hair, bright eyes and a grin that was sure to melt anyone's heart. It obviously melted Brittany's. "Nice to meet you, too," she said.

"Later," he said to Brittany, then hurried off to meet up with a couple of the older kids who were being bused to the school.

"He's great," she told Brittany.

"Seriously great," Brittany said, popping the sandwiches into a big basket. "He's tough, but he's got a good heart. I never knew that adoptions were so complicated, but Matt's worked it all out and we're going to have a huge party when it's final."

"I suspect he's worth all the work?"

"Absolutely." Brittany looked at her. "Is Jack bringing the little girl down today?"

She shrugged. "I don't know. I thought he was, but…" She checked the wall clock in the stainless-steel-and-enamel kitchen. Ten minutes to nine. "Maybe not." She crossed to wash her hands at the deep sinks. "He was looking for a nanny to take care of her, so maybe he found someone," she said. Or maybe he'd reconsidered having her around the child. She reached for a paper towel. Or maybe Eve had flown back up from Mexico.

She'd heard him just before she left for the center. She'd been sitting in the open window to the fire escape, sipping tea and relaxing. Then she'd heard his voice, low and intense on the thin morning air.

"I know, I know, they have things planned, but is there any way you can come up for a few days?"

Silence, an exhaled rush of air. "No, I'm not upset. I just wanted you to be here."

She'd started to ease the window down right then, but heard, "Eve, we're going to have to figure out—" before she'd clicked her window shut. But she couldn't forget that edge to his voice, that tinge of need that she was quite certain he'd never admit to.

She knew he was overwhelmed with everything in his life right then. She didn't need a degree to see that. The business mess. The child. And a personality that obviously took responsibility very seriously. Maybe Eve had known that, and maybe she'd agreed to fly up from Mexico to be with him and he was waiting at the loft for her to get there? She knew if she was in the same situation, she would have come back in a heartbeat. Then again, she wouldn't have been in Mexico in the first place.

Brittany was beside her at the sink rinsing out a glass, and said, "Well, I hope he finds someone to help him out with the little girl. Jack's definitely out of his league at the moment."

Rain stepped back, drying her hands and watching Brittany. "He's trying."

Brittany laid the glass on the drainer, then reached

for a paper towel to dry her hands. "That he is. That's all any of us can do, but I have to say, the image of Jack Ford with a child just boggles my mind. He's so work centered, so single-minded. Dad's been worried about him ever since his father died."

"He took the death hard?"

"I guess so, but that wasn't it. His father, from what I remember, messed things up around here pretty badly, and Jack stepped in to make things right."

She understood a bit more. "His father was…?" She couldn't think of a word to put there.

"His father was my father's best friend for years, in on the ground floor of this company, but he was a risk taker, who lived big, spent big and gambled big. When he died, they found out he'd been losing more than winning, and he left behind a huge mess." She picked up the box. "That's when Jack stepped in."

"It was that bad?"

"To the tune of costing LynTech two million plus."

More and more made sense about Jack. "What happened?"

"Jack made everything right." She shrugged. "And he looks after his mother, too, a strange woman who acts as if she was born to wealth." She tossed the used paper towel in the trash. "Well, he's not his father, that's for sure. Just look at what he's doing for that little girl. Clayton, his dad, wouldn't have ever done that. Even I thought he was an irresponsible, self-centered sort, and I've never been that focused on the business or my father's corporate friends."

That wasn't Jack at all. "There's always a fixer in a family and it sounds as if Jack's the fixer."

Brittany smiled. "You are a good doctor. That's exactly what Jack is. A fixer. He takes on everything and tries to fix it. He's a good man, but my father's a bit worried that he isn't stopping to smell the roses. I, personally, don't think he even knows there are roses."

Rain nodded. "Probably not."

Brittany pushed the door open with her hip. "See you later," she said. "And thanks for the help."

"No problem." Rain finished cleaning up, then went back into the main room. Nine o'clock and no Jack and Victoria. She went around a group of children having a story read to them under the main branch of the play tree and headed for the office. Mary stepped out just as she got to the door.

"Oh, Rain, just the person I wanted to see."

The lady was smiling, but not quite as genuine a smile as she seemed to always have. "Is there a problem?"

"Oh, my, no, just an inconvenience. Could you run upstairs and get Victoria? Mr. Ford…" She shrugged. "He's quite busy and he asked if someone could come and bring her down here. I think you're the best one to do that."

Rain was relieved that she'd see the child again today. "Where is she?"

"Mr. Terrell's office. She's with Rita Donovan."

"I'll go right up," she said and took off.

When she stepped through the door to Matthew Terrell's office, she found Victoria sitting on a chair pulled up to Rita's reception desk, drawing on a legal notepad. The child looked up, grabbed the old doll she'd laid on the desk by the papers, then scooted off the chair and came over to Rain. She looked up, ready to do whatever Rain asked of her. "Hi, munchkin." She looked at Rita. "You're doing above and beyond, aren't you?"

She shrugged philosophically. "My job description is constantly changing." Her smile was wry. "Watching her is one of the nicer things I'm asked to do around here."

"I bet it is," she said. "Do you know if she had breakfast?"

"Yes, as a matter of fact, she did. That's why everything's sort of…well, confused. Seems they stopped at a restaurant to get breakfast and…" She hesitated, then spelled out, "She had a tantrum over something about the doll." Then she went back to speaking. "I guess it was quite…stressful."

She felt Victoria tense slightly and she cut off the discussion. "We're going down to the center. Tell Mr. Ford we'll expect him around five."

"Of course," Rita said, then smiled at Victoria. "You have a great day."

Rain and Victoria went back down to the center, and for the whole day, Victoria never left Rain's side. They ate together, watched videos together, and Rain stayed with Victoria while she napped. But Rain could see a bit of the child emerging, or at least trying to. She saw the other kids playing with clay and when Rain offered it to her, she took it. Silently she went about playing with it, making balls and strange shapes, very intent on what she was doing.

Rain watched and talked to the child, a one-sided

conversation, yet there were responses. A nod, a shrug, even a slight smile when she was watching a cartoon about a sponge that came to life and lived under the sea. She was trying. She wanted to be happy. She wanted to be safe. Not much more than most people wanted, but as a child, she didn't have a clue how to get there, or if she could.

As it got closer to five, Rain kept an eye on the clock, hoping against hope that Jack would show up on time. He hadn't promised, but she did so hope that Rita told him and he took it to heart. At five minutes to the hour, she was sitting on the floor with Victoria on a huge protective tarp that was used when there was finger painting. Victoria delicately dipped her finger in a dark-blue paint, then lightly smeared it on the paper Rain had put in front of her.

"Nice color," Rain said as Victoria took more paint and made a bolder stroke on the paper. "Lovely. That's great."

The child became absorbed in her work, smearing blue everywhere, even on the overalls Rain had put on over her dress. But there was a freedom there that was trying to break through. She looked at Rain, then picked up some pink paint and held it out to her. "Me? You want me to paint? Oh, I'm not the talented one here, but my Dad is. He's a famous painter." The child's eyes widened slightly. "Maybe someday he'll paint you, maybe all in blue, or—" she took the pink paint "—maybe in pink."

"Pink?"

Rain was startled by the sound of Jack behind her. She looked up and back, and there he was, the three-piece suit, hair just so, and stress etched at his mouth and eyes. She twisted, got to her feet and faced him. "I was just telling Victoria that my father's a painter and maybe he could paint her sometime...maybe when he gets back from the Coast."

"I can see it now," he said with the hint of a wry smile, "Pink on pink on pink on pink."

She had to smile at that. That was her father's style now, but it hadn't always been that way and that wasn't what had made him famous in the art world. "Oh, he has his rational moments," she murmured. "Believe it or not."

"Thank God," Jack said, then looked at Victoria. "Time to go."

The little girl was on her feet, hands all blue, and blue smudging her face. Rain winced at the blob of blue paint on the foot of her doll. "Let me clean her up," she said and picked the little girl up, grabbed the doll and carried both of them into the kitchen. She put Victoria on the counter, and quickly cleaned her face, hands and finally the doll. She took the overalls off Victoria, then they went back into the main room. Jack was right there, nodded at the clean version of the little girl and looked at Mary as the older woman came across to them. "Would Victoria like a sucker to take home with her?" she asked, then looked at Jack, "Assuming it's okay with you?"

"Fine, no problem," he said.

Mary put her hand out to Victoria and said, "Then come along and we'll choose just the right one, and maybe get an extra one for later on."

Victoria hesitated, then shyly put her hand in Mary's and went to the other side of the room with her. That was when Jack turned to Rain. "How did it go today?"

"Probably better then breakfast," Rain said without thinking.

"So, Rita told you about that?"

"I'm sorry. We were just talking and she mentioned it."

He exhaled. "All I did was order her orange juice," and she got upset. She ended up spilling the glass on the table and crying this awful noiseless cry and clutching that doll as if I were going to take it away from her." He shook his head. "God knows what was wrong. She never gave me a clue."

"Orange juice?"

"Simple orange juice."

Rain didn't have a clue, either. "Well, it must have brought back some memory for her, something she couldn't deal with."

"That was my guess."

"How's she doing at the loft?"

"Okay. She met the cat this morning, and seemed to like him. Although he avoided her like the plague."

"He'll make up to her when he wants to."

Jack didn't want to talk about the cat. He didn't care about the damn cat. He cared about preventing another scene like they'd had that morning. "Will she ever talk?" he asked.

Rain didn't blink. "Of course."

"Of course? When?"

"When she wants to badly enough. She'll do what she wants to do, and you can't push her or rush her."

"Maybe that's your idea of parenting, it's not

mine. You don't just let a kid do whatever they want to do, whenever they want to do it. It doesn't work.''

''That wasn't what I was saying.''

They were toe-to-toe again, despite Jack's resolve to not get into anything with her. He had more on his mind than what she thought, and he didn't have the energy for this. ''Whatever,'' he murmured and looked away from her dark eyes to see where Victoria was.

But Rain caught his attention by putting her hand on his arm. He turned back to her. ''What?''

''I just meant that you have to take it easy and not expect too much.''

He heard her words, but his whole attention seemed to be on her fingers pressing against his jacket fabric that covered his forearm. ''Of course.''

She drew back. ''Whatever,'' she said, echoing his single word statement of moments earlier.

''Listen, I don't want to argue. I just want Victoria to be all right.''

''Of course you do, and you're doing it alone.''

Why did that sound like a slam against Eve? ''I'm doing it.''

''Sure you are and you're—''

''Tense?'' he supplied, knowing where she was going before she got there. ''I know, I know,'' he said.

''Well, you are, and Victoria can feel it, too. George and Bree made very sure when I was little that they didn't share their problems with me.''

''Bree?''

''My mother.''

''Well, they sound like saints.''

That was so sarcastic and he hadn't meant it to be,

not really. And he hated the way she drew back from him. This woman made him feel even more tense. "They aren't, and never claimed to be," she said, her cheeks touched by a hint of color. "But they loved me and did the very best they could for me. I never doubted that."

He couldn't believe it, but at that moment, he almost felt jealous of what she must have had in her childhood. Security, love, care. He'd lived with being the one to pick up the pieces, over and over again. "I'm doing the best I can with Victoria."

"I know you are," she said softly.

He didn't want this, "Gee, you're a good person," either. When it came to Rainbow Swan Armstrong, he really didn't know what he wanted. Then she touched her tongue to her lips and a thought came to him that he pushed aside quickly, overlapping with the flashing memory of that moment when he'd kissed her. No, he didn't want any complications. He had enough in his life at the moment, and letting himself think of her in any terms besides neighbor or therapist was a huge mistake, one he wouldn't make again.

Chapter Eight

"I need to get going," Jack said abruptly, as Victoria reentered the room with Mary. The child had two suckers in her hand, one yellow, one red, and the doll in the other. "Ready to go?" he asked her.

Victoria went over to him and waited. He nodded to Mary, then looked at Rain. She was looking at him oddly, as if she knew something about him that even he didn't know. He'd about decided that she read minds, but it wasn't that. If she could read his mind, she would have done more then blushed. She probably would have slapped him.

"I'll bring her tomorrow, if that's all right?"

"That's perfect," Mary said. "Just wonderful."

"See you tomorrow," Rain said to Victoria, then looked at Jack. "I'll be here."

He started to leave, feeling as though he were escaping something he didn't understand or want to. And it didn't leave even when he was in the company car and heading away from LynTech. He'd thought of stopping to eat on the way home, but Victoria's outburst that morning had him telling the driver to go directly to the loft.

Two hours later, Victoria was in her nightgown, watching cartoons on the television, the cat watching her warily from his perch on the half wall, and Jack was at the computer. The three of them in the same space and all separate, Jack thought as he frowned at the figures on the computer screen. Not exactly a homey feeling.

The phone rang and he reached for it. "Hello?"

"Jack, it's Zane. I was going to try to get back to you this afternoon after the meeting, but Lindsey had a doctor's appointment and things got lost in the shuffle."

"What's going on?"

"I've decided, and Matt agrees, to lay our cards on the table with Sommers, tell him the truth and if he goes for it, he goes for it. If he doesn't, we back out and let it go."

"And then?"

"We move on, find out how the information got out, and start looking at other options."

All this was for nothing? "Just walk away?"

"If the rest of the board agrees to it."

"Bad idea," Jack said.

"How so?"

"It shows weakness, indecisiveness. You name it."

"So, we ram it through and push Sommers to fall in step?"

Jack couldn't imagine pushing E. J. Sommers to do anything he didn't want to do. "We make another offer, dress it up a bit, and stand behind it, then make sure it isn't undermined."

"Sounds good, but how do you plan on doing that?"

"We'll work it out."

"If we let it go, Jack, you can walk now. You can go back to London."

Was that a bribe? A way to make him agree? "I won't be here much longer than another week anyway." He couldn't believe he wasn't grasping at the escape. "How about it? Stick it out?"

There was silence, then Zane said, "Okay. We'll figure out another deal, then tackle Sommers from a different angle."

"If he's not off somewhere having a good time."

"That's a problem. I don't know how he gets anything done the way he lives. Oh, speaking of living. I'm not going to be in tomorrow. Lindsey needs me at some classes she's going to take."

"I thought she was sick?"

"That's what I thought, but she's sure she can do this. Natural childbirth, and that means a coach and that means me." He laughed roughly. "I just hope to hell I don't faint dead away at the most important moment. Matt's going to cover for me tomorrow, so you two start, maybe talk to Robert, too. Call if you need me, but otherwise, I'll see you in a day or so."

Jack hung up and then stood, stretched his hands over his head, and turned. The cat scooted past him, up on the work table, over to the windows, then leaped to the highest point and was gone through the open transom. He looked at Victoria, but she hadn't moved, and he realized it was because she'd fallen asleep. He crossed and turned off the cartoons that flashed on the television, then went over to her small bed and got it ready for her and carried her to it.

She barely stirred when he put her down, curling

onto her side and never losing her grip on the ever present doll. Her cheek rested on the doll's head, and she sighed slightly. She looked tiny and vulnerable and, he had to admit, softly sweet. Jack stood back, exhaled and went into the kitchen to get something to drink. Nothing. Rita's assistant had stocked the refrigerator with juice, milk, even bottled water, but not a drop of alcohol in the place. He finally took a bottle of water, went back to the computer and got more comfortable. He undid his shirt, untucked it, and stepped out of his shoes.

He went back to work, and when the buzzer for the entry door sounded, it startled him. He looked up at the clock. Midnight? He got up and crossed when it buzzed again. He glanced at Victoria, but she was sound asleep. He reached for the button, leaning close to the box so he didn't have to speak too loudly. "Yes?"

"Oh, great, I was worried you weren't there or you'd be asleep. It's me, Rain."

He would have recognized that voice anywhere, even over the old speaker box. "What are you doing buzzing me at this time of night?"

"Well, it's a long story, but…I'm locked out. Can you buzz me in?"

He hit the button, then a moment later, he heard the old elevator start up. He opened the door and looked into the corridor as the lift lumbered up to the second floor. Then he saw Rain. He'd thought she'd gone out to dinner or something, but he knew that wasn't the case when he realized that all she had on was another version of her tie-dyed sleep shirt. This one was a fluorescent peach color with splashes of green mingled with royal blues.

As the elevator stopped, he wondered how any woman could wear colors like that and look so good. No makeup. Her hair loose and falling down her back. She lifted the door on the elevator and stepped out. And bare feet. He wasn't aware he was smiling until she stepped out of the elevator and said, "It's not funny," she muttered.

"Then what is it?" he asked as he leaned one shoulder on the door frame.

"It's a..." She bit her lip and turned to put the cage door back down.

"It's midnight," he said.

She turned. "And your point is...?"

"Most people are in their homes at this time of night, or they're dressed and out having a good time."

She crossed her arms over her breasts and it made the T-shirt rise a bit more, showing even more of her legs. "Okay, since I've never claimed to be normal, and I'm sure you wouldn't think I was even if I was in a formal gown coming back from the ball, I dropped something off the fire escape. I went down the stairs, but I couldn't find it, and when I tried to go back up the stairs—" she shrugged "—I couldn't reach them."

"What?"

"I jumped the last bit and never thought that they were too high for me reach when I wanted to go back."

"What did you drop?"

She grimaced. "I dropped the cat."

"You what?" Jack asked, straightening up.

"For someone who claims not to like the beast, that got your attention," she muttered. "But, don't worry. He's just fine. Probably used up more than one of his nine lives, but he's unscathed."

"You pushed him off the fire escape?"

She rolled her eyes up as if in supplication. "Of course not. Not on purpose. I was sitting there, just meditating, and he surprised me. I yelled, he jumped, and he went through the side rail and plunged down two stories." She came closer. "I lowered the stairs, went down, nervous about what I'd find." She shook her head. "He was sitting there cleaning himself when I found him. The rotten…"

Now he was smiling. "And you couldn't reach the stairs to come back up?"

"You got it. One of the banes of being a short person and not remembering that they don't go down all the way sometimes."

"You're lucky you didn't find a drunk down there," he said, his smile slipping a bit when he realized how vulnerable she had to have been all alone in the dark. "You shouldn't have gone down there like that."

"What was I going to do? If he was hurt, he'd be dead by the time it was daylight, and I couldn't come and get you and say, 'Get the cat, but don't tell me if he's flat as a pancake.'" She shrugged. "I'm okay. Thanks for letting me in." She glanced past him. "How's the munchkin?"

"Asleep."

"Any problems tonight?"

"Not really. We came right back here and she watched cartoons, then fell asleep."

"That's great. She's doing better."

"I hope so."

She shifted from foot to foot. "Well, I guess I'll head back to my loft." Then she closed her eyes and exhaled in a rush. "Oh, darn, darn, darn," she muttered under her breath.

"What is it now?"

She opened her eyes. "I'm locked out. The loft's locked up tight. George never locks it, but I...I can't get back in."

"The ladder's still down?"

"Yes."

"Okay, come on in, and I'll go down my ladder, go up yours, open your door, then let you in."

"Oh, no, you can't do—"

"You can't, not unless you're going to grow a few inches to reach the ladder."

She sighed. "Okay, okay, I'd appreciate it."

They went inside. He crossed to the escape window, took the tie he had wrapped around the handle off, then opened it. He stepped out onto the landing, then turned back to Rain. She was a little more than three feet from him, softened by shadows and it reminded him of the first night. "Pull my stairs back up when I'm down," he said, then moved to release them.

Rain followed him onto the landing, and he felt her watching him climb down into the shadows. He hit the ground, went to her stairs, jumped, grabbed them, then went up. He got to the landing and looked across at Rain. "Pull my stairs up, and I'll be right there," he said, then went into her loft. He went straight through and out into the hallway, then knocked softly on his front door.

She was there, opening it for him. "Done," he said in a whisper as he stepped back inside.

"Thanks," she said.

He closed the door and went to the couch and sank down on it. "No problem. Just don't go climbing down there again at night. Okay?"

She stood over him. He knew she wanted to protest the request, but she didn't. Instead, she said, "I owe you."

"No, you don't," he said, grimacing as he rubbed his hand across the back of his neck.

"You hurt yourself?" she asked, crouching in front of him, her face puckered with real concern.

"What? Oh, no, just…" He exhaled and flexed his shoulders. "I've been working and it's after midnight."

"You really need to—"

"Don't start," he murmured.

"Let me help?"

The idea of a massage from her was way too seductive. "No massages," he murmured.

"Okay, no massage." Then she snapped her fingers, got up and said over her shoulder, "I'll be right back."

She went out, leaving the door ajar, and he heard her go into her loft. Less than a minute later, she was back, closing the door quietly and coming over to him. He looked up and she had two glasses in one hand and a decanter filled with a dark liquid in the other.

She held them up. "I think you could use this."

"Alcohol?" he asked, sounding just a bit hopeful.

"Brandy, I think."

He shook his head. "I thought you said that alcohol didn't help."

"I don't think it does, but if it gives you the impression that it does, then impressions are sometimes more important than fact." She poured their drinks then sank down on the couch beside him.

"Where was this the other night when you gave me that tea?" he asked.

"Actually, I forgot about it until now. It's George's and you can consider it medicinal, if you like."

Jack took a sip. It was brandy, and not just any brandy. It was excellent. He took another sip to make sure, then rested his glass on his thigh. "Do you have any idea what this is?"

Rain had curled up in the corner, tucking her legs under her and cradling the glass in both hands. "I wouldn't know. As I said, it's George's. He probably sold a painting and wanted to celebrate."

Jack took another drink, then said, "He sells them for money?"

She shrugged. "He sure does, much to his chagrin. Filthy lucre, I think he calls it. But he takes it and people love his work."

"You're serious?"

She fingered her glass and actually smiled slightly, an endearing expression that he thoroughly enjoyed. "Sir, have you ever heard of an artist called Dune? One word, and the name's hidden in his paintings?"

He shrugged. "Maybe, I don't know."

"Well, a lot of people have heard of him, and they

pay a good deal of money to have one of his works. Some collect them. Dune is George Armstrong. My father.''

He shook his head. From the free-form color works he'd seen, he would have thought the man would have to bribe someone to take his work home. ''You're kidding?''

''No, not at all. Next time you go into the main entrance of LynTech, look at the two paintings on the wall to the left. That's his work.''

He vaguely remembered representational canvases there. ''He actually paints real things?''

''Perfectly, but…as one critic said, 'with passion and heart,' and I think that critic bought one of his works.'' She took a small sip of the alcohol and grimaced. ''I don't know much about art or about brandy.'' She motioned to his drink. ''Is it helping?''

''I think so.'' He wouldn't say that he loved the way her image was softening in front of him, the way the knot in his middle was easing, or that he actually liked just sitting here with her.

''Good. If you don't figure out how to relax, you're bound to implode. You can't keep pushing yourself just to prove that you're…'' Her words faded off, leaving the statement hanging between them.

''That I'm what?'' he asked.

''Nothing.'' She sipped some more brandy. ''Did I say thank you for rescuing me.''

''I can't stand that,'' Jack said.

''What? Rescuing me?''

''No, the way you're almost bursting to say something, then you don't.''

"Sorry, I always think that people will feel I'm analyzing them or something if I say too much."

"Well, that didn't stop you before. Why change now?"

"Okay, I was going to say that you're the type who always has to make things right, that you take all the pressure and the burden on yourself. And that's tiring to say the least."

"And how did you get this insight into what I am?"

"Am I wrong?"

"No, you're not."

"Are you an only child?"

"Yes."

"Me, too. Why didn't your parents have more kids?"

He was taken off guard by the question. He'd never understood much about his parents except his mother never faced reality and his father never faced what he did. As far as having more kids? He finished his brandy and leaned forward to pour another glass for himself.

"I don't know," he said as he sat back. "Maybe they didn't want them. Or maybe they couldn't have them. They never said, and I didn't ask."

"Really? I asked my parents for a sister or a brother every birthday and every Christmas."

"And?"

"I got clothes and toys and candy. No sibling. And, boy, was I disappointed."

"Why didn't they have more?"

"George told me once that I was enough. That one Rainbow Swan filled his world, then he changed the subject. My theory is they never had more because they couldn't figure out what to do with more kids. By the time I was eight, Bree lived near San Francisco, and George was out here. I went back and forth and so did they, but if there were more kids involved, they couldn't have made it work.''

"They never thought of all of you living in one city and in one house?''

"Oh, until I was eight, we were together, not in one city all the time, and goodness knows, not in one house. But together. Then Bree took me to the Coast. That's where she was from and where she met George.''

"Let me guess, Haight Ashbury?''

She didn't seem to notice the tinge of sarcasm in the question. "As a matter of fact, yes, at a rally.''

"What happened when you were eight?''

"I don't know, but suddenly we were on the Coast and George was here, and we had our 'adventures' coming to see him, and he had his treks out to see us.''

"That's some marriage,'' he murmured.

"Oh, they aren't married. I mean, they said their vows in the forest up by Big Sur four or five years before I showed up, but they were never really married.''

He chuckled softly. Why wasn't he surprised? "They're still making the trips back and forth?''

"That's where George is now, seeing Bree.'' She sipped more brandy. "When I was little, I always thought that I was the one who forced Bree to settle down, but I think that deep down, she wanted to be in one place, in a familiar home. George never wanted that, so I was the excuse.''

''That's quite an arrangement,'' Jack said.

''It worked. It's still working. They love each other in their own way. As George says, 'Marriage is in the spirit, not in fact.'''

''You believe that?''

''Well, they've been together a heck of a lot longer than most people, so it must work. And I like the idea of people being together because they want to, rather than being legally forced to be together.'' She sighed. ''I just bet you had a totally traditional childhood.''

Jack didn't have a clue why he was telling her anything, but he heard himself say, ''Two parents. One child. A huge house. Mother had her clubs and social circle. She still does.''

''What about your father?''

He laughed, a short barking laugh with little humor in it and took another drink before he answered her. ''I had one of those, I think. Mostly he was in and out, making business deals, spending money, making more business deals. He died ten years ago, the same year I came on at LynTech.'' He finished off his brandy and reached for the bottle again. He poured himself some more, then offered her another drink. She shook her head, then he sat back. ''I don't remember a whole lot about Clayton Ford.''

''I'm sorry,'' she said softly.

''It's been a long time.''

''Sure, but I can't imagine not having George in my life. I don't know what I'd do without him.''

He wished he'd felt that way about his father. ''Well, my father wasn't exactly Father of the Year material.'' He swallowed more brandy, and the words were tumbling out before he could stop them. ''Hell, he wasn't even a father at all.''

He knew he'd crossed a line when he heard her gasp softly. ''I can't believe you mean that.''

''Oh, don't start analyzing me. You never knew Clayton Ford. Hell, I never knew him. When he died, he left a mess for me to clean up and it took forever.''

''What kind of mess?'' she asked.

He looked at her, the brandy mellowing everything in him except her affect on him. ''Money. Robert took him into LynTech, and he was there long enough to drain almost two million out of the company.''

''He embezzled money?''

He grabbed the brandy bottle and splashed more of the liquid into his glass. He took a bigger drink than he should have, then muttered, ''Hell, no, he thought he was a brilliant businessman, even if his methods were less than upstanding, and he manipulated things so that a lot of LynTech's capital was put into a scheme he'd set up. When he died, Robert Lewis was left holding the bag and the proof.''

''Mr. Lewis told you about it?''

''Hell, no, Robert never said a thing to me about it.'' He tossed off more brandy. ''I never would have known what my father did, if I hadn't found his papers when I was trying to figure out his estate. I found out two things. First, that my mother and father were almost flat broke when he died, that they were living on a bubble of goodwill from a lot of different people, but Robert mostly. Then I found the papers about his underhanded dealings. That's when I knew what he was and what he'd done to LynTech.''

"So, you stepped in to fix it?" she asked softly.

"God, you're a psychic, too," he muttered, taking another drink of the alcohol and letting the fire spread in his middle before he went on bitterly. "Sure thing. Good old Jack to the rescue. I stepped in and tried to make up for what my father did."

"Did you?"

"I've tried."

"After ten years, you have to have done a lot more than that."

He poured a bit more brandy and sank back on the couch. "Oh, moneywise, we're more than even, but I owe Robert more than that. He could have brought charges against my family when he found out. He could have destroyed my mother and me. Instead, he kept quiet and let me do what I had to do and he never mentioned it again. He let me work my way up in the company, and he trusted me. He didn't have any reason to, but he did."

"What about your mother?"

"Oh, she wore black for a whole year, then she got on with her life as if nothing had happened."

"You take care of her?"

"I made investments for her, and she lives off them now."

"Jack to the rescue," she whispered.

He looked at her, her image not as clear as it had been earlier, and lifted his glass. "You got it," he mumbled, with no idea why he was telling her so much. Then again, it was probably the brandy. He drained his glass then settled deeper into the cushion of the couch and closed his eyes.

Rain watched Jack relax and knew, after just a few

minutes, that he was asleep. It was the first time she'd seen him not looking so tense, and the difference was remarkable. His words had torn at her. She didn't know how he'd done what he'd done. Losing his father, then having to fix everything. And now there was Victoria. The man was amazing. "Jack to the rescue," she whispered. When she sat forward to place her glass on the table, Jack moved and put his hand on her arm.

She turned to him, and it seemed incredibly natural to slip over and sink into him. His arm circled her, pulling her to his chest, and she felt him exhale on a shudder. "God, I don't know why…" His voice was slightly thick from the alcohol.

"Why, what?" she asked, closing her eyes tightly when she felt his heart beating against her cheek.

"Why you're you," he mumbled, then exhaled, and his arm around her felt heavy. He sighed, and his breathing was deep and even. Once again, he was asleep.

She sat there for a very long time. Then she made herself ease forward and stand. Jack resettled without waking and Rain looked down at him. He seemed almost peaceful, and the anger that she'd felt toward Eve only deepened. Eve should be here. She should be listening to Jack. Drinking brandy with him. Just holding him and letting him hold on to her. Rain reached out, brushing at an errant lock of hair that had fallen across his forehead, then bent down and kissed his brow.

"Sleep well," she whispered, then quietly left his apartment.

Chapter Nine

Jack woke to a raging headache and the sound of explosions all around him. He opened his eyes, closing them immediately when bright light streaming in from the windows hit him full-force. He pressed a hand to his head, then opened his eyes just a slit and tried to focus. He was in the loft. He knew that. But the noise? He eased his head to the right and saw that the television was on. It was showing a cartoon in which a cat was chasing a mouse and shooting something that looked like a bazooka at the rodent.

The noises made him flinch, then he saw Victoria. The child was still in her nightgown, holding her doll, watching the cartoons. She must have turned the television on herself. He tried to sit up, forcing himself upright, enduring the pain from the action. He saw the two glasses on the table. One half-full. One completely empty. And the brandy decanter, almost empty now.

He hadn't passed out from drinking since college. He remembered Rain talking, then him talking, saying things he couldn't remember, but knew he shouldn't have said. Then a vague memory of Rain being in his arms. A dream? God, he couldn't remember. The explosions on the television made him flinch.

"Victoria?" he managed to croak, his voice raspy, and his throat dry. The child turned at the sound of her name.

"Good morning. I'm going to take a shower and get dressed, then I'll get you some breakfast," he said, making himself stand and find his balance, which wasn't an easy thing to do. "You watch the cartoons, okay?"

She turned back to the cartoons and he assumed that was a yes. He made his way into the bathroom and emerged from the steamy room fifteen minutes later feeling almost human. That had been good brandy, damn good brandy, and not something anyone in their right mind would use to get drunk. But that was exactly what he'd done. He'd kept drinking until he was out of it, until he was on the couch, and Rain had kissed him.

Jack stopped too fast, and paid for it when pain radiated behind his eyes. She'd kissed him? No, he'd imagined it, that soft contact on his forehead as if she'd been tucking in a small child. Hallucinations. That sure shot down the theory that the better the brandy, the better you did afterward. He was a wreck. He went right to the coffeemaker, started it, then looked for something to make for breakfast. He wasn't taking the chance of going out again, especially in the shape he was in.

WHEN RAIN FINALLY awoke that morning, she was shocked to see the sun was up. She'd slept so poorly since coming to Houston. In fact, she'd spent more time on the fire-escape landing than in her bed. But last night, after returning from Jack's loft, she'd easily fallen into a deep sleep.

Now, after showering and dressing in jeans, a pink tank top and sandals, she grabbed her bag and left. Jack's door was closed and there were no signs of life from inside, at least that she could tell.

She hurried down and headed for LynTech, hoping to arrive before Victoria showed up at the center. But given the fact that the clock in her car read nine o'clock, she didn't think that was a rational hope. When she walked into the center, she waved to Mary who was helping two other workers set up a craft time, and looked around for Victoria. But there was no tiny, quiet blond-haired child to be seen.

She waited until Mary was done with her part in play time, then motioned the older woman over to where she stood, near the kitchen. "Where is she?" Rain said as Mary got closer.

The lady smiled. "Victoria?"

"Yes," she said, wondering why it was so hard for her to smile.

"I believe she's up with Ms. Donovan in Mr. Terrell's office. She wouldn't stay here because you weren't here. I was just going to call and see if you were coming in at all."

"I overslept," she admitted. "I'll go and get Victoria, then be right back down."

"Wonderful," Mary said.

Rain went up to the top floor and hurried to Matthew Terrell's office. But when she opened the door to go in, she found herself facing Jack. The last time she'd seen him, he was rather drunk and sleeping peacefully. Now the man looked dead sober, and far from peaceful. Maybe a bit hungover, although George had sworn you could drink as much brandy as you wanted, and it wouldn't cause a hangover. Obviously he'd been wrong.

Or, maybe Jack was the exception. He looked rather grim, and not terribly happy. But despite all that, she couldn't ignore the fact that she was drawn to him at that moment, the same way she'd been drawn to him last night, compelling her to kiss his forehead. She could remember the feel of his skin on her lips, that heat. She caught herself, bringing her thoughts up short. She really didn't want to go down that road.

"I—I was looking for you," she said quickly. "I mean, really looking for Victoria, not you, but Victoria." She had no idea why she was stammering so badly.

"Well, you found us," he said. His voice held a hint of hoarseness.

Victoria peeked shyly around Jack, then she actually stepped forward and almost smiled. It did Rain's heart good to see her acting almost like a normal child and wearing a pair of overalls. "Do you want to come down and play today?" she asked.

Without hesitation, the little girl took Rain's offered hand, clutching her doll the other. Rain felt her heart lurch when the tiny fingers held to hers so trustingly. She looked back at Jack. "What time will you be down?"

He exhaled roughly. "The nanny is coming by this evening to meet Victoria. Then she'll start tomorrow."

''When's she coming?''

''She said sometime around eight. I'll be down to get Victoria around five.''

''That's fine.''

''Good,'' he said, and moved out into the corridor, forcing her and Victoria to step back and give him room. Without a word he headed down the hall and they fell in step beside him on their way to the elevator.

''The cat?'' she said.

He cast her a slanting look. ''What about the cat?''

''Did you see him this morning?''

''He showed for food,'' he muttered. ''He always shows for food.''

''I guess he's okay, then,'' Rain said as she stopped with Victoria at the elevator doors. ''No damage?''

''He's fine for the moment,'' Jack muttered ominously, then smiled at Victoria. ''Bye, bye. See you later,'' he said and headed away from them to go farther down the hallway.

''See you at five,'' Rain called after him, then let go of Victoria's hand to push the call button. When she turned to the child, she was stunned to see her hand up, showing five fingers. Rain darted a look down the corridor, but Jack was gone. She crouched in front of the little girl. ''Five?''

Victoria nodded.

''Yes, five. Uncle Jack will come and get you at five o'clock,'' she said, and gave in to the urge to hug Victoria to her. ''That's wonderful,'' she said softly.

FIVE O'CLOCK CAME and went, and Jack couldn't get out of his meeting to contact Rain. When he finally was able to leave, he walked out of the conference room and stopped when he heard Rain's voice.

The others in the meeting went out around him, but he stayed very still, listening.

"Okay, it's all up to me. If I'm very careful, very, very careful, and if I don't sneeze, I might just be able to do this," she said in that voice.

He glanced in the direction of the side room off of the entry to the conference room and heard her say, "I think maybe I can do this."

Then there was a crashing sound, wood against wood, and Rain laughing. He was stunned at the response her voice pulled from him, how any words she said turned seductive, and her laugh... He took a deep breath, then looked inside the room. Rain was sitting on the floor with Victoria and a mess of wooden blocks were scattered between them. Rain was grinning, and she touched Victoria on the hand that clutched her doll. "I've been skunked!"

When she looked up, the smile faded just a bit, but that didn't diminish its effect on Jack. He'd had a long, miserable day trying to convince the others not to give up on the EJS acquisition. The sight of the two of them was like a ray of sunshine after a long, dark storm. Before he could analyze the whys of his reactions, he said, "Skunked?" and Victoria looked up at him as he came closer to where they sat on the carpeting.

Rain got up in one smooth motion, brushing her hands on her jeans. "Skunked, as in beaten. Losing big time."

"Oh, that skunked," he said. "Victoria skunked you?"

"Big time," she said, looking away from him to watch the little girl get up and stand between them.

"What are you doing up here, besides getting skunked?"

"Waiting for you." The smile was almost gone now. "You said five and it's—" she looked past him "—five-fifteen."

"The meeting ran a little longer than I expected," he said.

"I thought we'd come up here and wait as it closed in on five. Rita said you were in a conference, so we got blocks and we waited."

"Well, I'm out now. Thanks for bringing her up."

"Sure. We had a good day."

He was thrilled that someone did. "Good, good." He looked down at Victoria. "Ready to go? The nanny is going to come by tonight to meet you, so we need to get home and get ready."

He was startled when Victoria reached for Rain's hand and held on to her doll with the other. He didn't know what he'd expected, but it wasn't this.

Rain glanced at him, then crouched in front of her. "What's wrong?"

Victoria looked at Jack and frowned, then back at Rain, but she didn't say a thing. "It's time to go, sweetie," she said. "You're going to go to the loft and you're going to meet your new nanny, and maybe Uncle Jack will let you watch some television."

Victoria looked up at her, then to Jack, but didn't move.

"Victoria, we need to leave," he said.

"I told you we were coming up to meet Uncle Jack so he could take you home," Rain said.

The child listened to her, then shook her head, a very emphatic no.

Rain looked up at Jack and he knew she was waiting for him to take over, but he didn't have any suggestions, short of picking her up and taking her with him by force. But he had a gut feeling that wasn't a good idea. He thought his day had gone badly because of too much brandy and not enough good sleep, but right then he knew it wasn't a hangover that was the problem. He needed to get out of here, and breathe some air.

"Victoria, we need to leave."

But Victoria didn't give in. She held her ground, silent, yet stronger at that moment than both adults. He exhaled, and Rain stood to face him, putting it all on him for what happened next. "What do you want to do? It's up to you."

"What are my choices?"

"I can explain things to her, that you two have to leave and why, which will take some time and might not work. Or you can let it go this one time and I'll drive back to the loft with you. I can leave my car and get it tomorrow."

Trapped. That's what he was, trapped by a four-year-old, but he didn't have the time or energy to fight right then. He glanced down at Victoria who flashed him a look that could have been pleading or defiant. He didn't know. "I hate to ask you for anything else," he said to Rain.

"It's not a problem."

Jack locked eyes with Rain and in that moment, he knew he wanted to hear her voice a bit longer, to drink it in and forget about this mess at LynTech. "Okay, let's go," he said, and Victoria almost smiled.

VICTORIA SAT BETWEEN Rain and Jack in the back of the company car in a booster seat. The minute they were settled, Jack's phone rang. He answered it, said, "Put him on," and began speaking Japanese.

Rain sank back, looking around the luxury car, then glanced down at Victoria. The little girl held her doll with one hand and pressed her other hand to her stomach. "Victoria?" she said, and the child looked at her. "Are you hungry?"

The little girl frowned at her, pursing her lips together.

Rain motioned to Jack to get his attention. "What is it?"

"She's hungry."

He looked as if she'd said, "She's flying." "What?"

"Hungry. Food. Victoria's hungry."

"Oh, sure, of course," he said, then motioned to the front of the car. "Ask the driver to stop at a restaurant. We have time before the nanny shows up."

"Where do you want to go?"

He looked impatient at even having to think about it. "Wherever. You choose." He motioned to the driver. "Harold, take her anywhere she wants," and the man nodded. Then Jack was back on his call.

"We—we need to stop to eat," she said to the driver.

He looked at her in the mirror. "Where do you want to go?"

Jack had told her to choose, so she would. "Just a

minute,'' she said and looked down at Victoria. ''What do you want for dinner?''

She didn't expect, or get, a verbal response. What she did get was a slight shrug.

It was going to be a guessing game. ''Okay, let's see. Steak?''

A frown.

''Pizza?''

Not quite as much of a frown, but no smile.

''Okay, how about spaghetti?''

The frown was gone and she didn't smile, but Rain took it as agreement. She knew just the place, a restaurant George had told her about a few years ago, one she went to every time she was in town. ''Do you know Our Place?''

''No, ma'am.''

She told him where it was located, then sat back and said to Victoria, ''We are going to a really cool restaurant. They've got the best spaghetti in the world and this great bread and really nice people.'' Victoria didn't look impressed, but she didn't frown, either. She saw Jack's hand clench on his thigh as she spoke to Victoria. ''We'll have a good dinner.''

After a few minutes, the car slowed, and Rain looked out the side window, recognizing the narrow street and the rows of small shops and businesses that lined it. Most were closed for the night, but a few were still open, including the restaurant near the end of the street. It had once been an old store and was now a whole foods restaurant. The blacked-out windows were fronted by potted trees, and a huge sign high above the parking area between the building and the street, flashing the name in a shocking fluorescent green. Under the name a sign announced, Good Food From The Earth For Good People.

The car pulled into the parking lot and parked near the entry. A cobbled walk led to the doors. Jack put his phone back in his pocket and looked out the window. "Where in the hell are we?" he asked.

"The restaurant," Rain said, noticing how exhausted Jack looked.

The driver opened the door, but instead of getting out, Jack looked at Rain. "I'm not hungry."

"Victoria wants spaghetti, which, as a matter of fact, is their specialty, whole grain, great marinara sauce and homemade bread. And you need to eat."

He shook his head. "You two go and eat and I'll get some work done out here."

She wasn't going to let him do this. He didn't need more work, and for reasons she didn't want to look at too closely, she wanted him to relax and let go of his work for a while. "No."

"Excuse me?"

"No, you come in with us or we don't go in." It was a bluff. "So, what's it going to be?"

Victoria looked from Jack to Rain, then back at Jack. "I've got work—"

"Don't we all," she murmured, cutting off his excuse. "But it's dinnertime, and it's good to eat together." She lowered her voice and said, "Besides, I'm not a…" She hesitated, then spelled the word *baby-sitter*. She felt Victoria squirm a bit, and she tried to make her tone less tense. "Why can't you just relax, have a meal, then get back to your work?"

He frowned at her, obviously not happy, but he didn't argue anymore. He just got out, and she and the child followed. She could tell he wasn't happy, but she'd take his agreement any way it came. The three of them went to the doors, and stepped into the greeting area of the restaurant.

The first time she'd been here, she'd been surprised at the interior of the place. Instead of the steel, glass and stone outside, the interior was like a home. The foyer had brick walls, a wood floor and plants everywhere. Arches on either side of a wonderful painting of Hawaii led to a divided dining area that gave the whole place a cozy feel. The doors swung shut, and the owner, a tall, lean man, maybe sixty or so, with snow-white hair caught back from his weathered face in a ponytail, appeared. His clothes were as informal as the restaurant, a Hawaiian shirt ablaze with pinks, greens and blues, and cutoff Levi's worn with thong sandals. Sylvester Johnson was never called Sylvester. He went by the name of Lizard, something to do with his Hawaiian sojourns. She'd never found out the exact origins of the name.

He saw them, and smiled hugely. "Welcome to Our Place," he said, then noticed Rain. "Oh, Rainbow, I didn't know you were in town! Terrific!"

He hugged her while he said, "Greetings, greetings." When he looked at Victoria, his smile grew. "What a beauty," he said, crouching in front of her. "And what's your name, peanut?"

She watched him wide-eyed, but she didn't recoil. She didn't speak to him, either.

"Victoria," Rain said.

"Victoria, a beautiful name," he said, then stood and looked at Jack. Really looked at Jack. At the three-piece suit, the expensive shirt and leather shoes.

Rain saw the slight surprise in his expression, and inwardly thought that Lizard was a bit of a snob himself. But he smiled easily at Jack and held out his hand. "I'm Lizard," he said, "This is my place and you're very welcome."

Jack shook the man's hand, and simply said, "Jack Ford."

"Well, come on in," Lizard said, and motioned them to follow him as he picked up some menus from a side table. "I've got the best table in the house for you all," he said, and headed to the archway on the right.

They stepped into a side room, a thirty-by-thirty-foot space with a stone fountain with three dolphins in the center, and tables set around it. He took them to a table farthest from the entry, and the only one by a window.

They sat and Lizard asked what they wanted to drink. "Got some great cabernet, a small vineyard, lovely bouquet, organic grapes," he said, then tapped Victoria on the head. "But for you, we have a special milk, a great year." Victoria nodded to him.

"Milk it is," he said, then looked at Jack. "How about you?"

"The wine's fine," Jack said, and Rain agreed.

After Lizard left, Victoria very carefully set her doll on the one empty seat beside her. It was the first time Rain had seen her willingly put the doll down and leave it one place. More surprises for the day. And it gave her hope that whatever was going on inside the child was passing, and could be dealt with.

"Victoria, how about that spaghetti?"

The child looked at her, and gave that almost imperceptible nod she'd mastered, then sat back in her chair and clasped her hands in her lap. Rain glanced at Jack who hadn't even opened his menu. "What are you going to have?" she asked him.

His phone rang and he reached for it, flipping it open. "Yes?"

He listened for a long moment, then held it away from his ear and said, "I have to take this."

"How long will it take?" she asked, angrily.

"Five, ten minutes tops," he said.

"Five minutes," she said, looking at her watch before meeting his gaze again. "Agreed?"

He exhaled. "You drive a hard bargain."

"You have no idea," she said softly.

He got up, strode across the room and through the arch. "He'll be right back," Rain told Lizard when the man returned with their drinks.

"A businessman?" he said, putting the milk in front of Victoria, then pouring wine in goblets for Jack and Rain.

"Oh, yes," she said on a sigh.

"Have to say, I'm a bit surprised, Rainbow. But you never know. You shouldn't judge people by how they look. I'm living proof of that."

Rain nodded. "Absolutely."

"What are you going to have tonight?"

She looked at the door and there was no sign of Jack, but she was starving and she knew Victoria was hungry, too. "What do you say we order for Uncle Jack?" she asked the girl, then put in their orders.

Jack was back in what she would have guessed was exactly five minutes, but she didn't check her watch. He sat down, reached for his wineglass and took a drink. As he set it back on the table, he glanced at Rain. "You've been here a lot?"

"Off and on, whenever I'm in town visiting George."

"The owner's a friend of George's?" he asked.

"Just because they both have ponytails and bad taste in clothes, you assume that they're friends," she said with a smile to soften the words. "Actually, they are, but it's not their clothes or hair that brought them together, or any hippie commune."

He lifted his wineglass. "Are you going to tell me what did bring them together?"

"Surfing," she said with a smile as a waitress appeared with their food. "Hanging ten in Hawaii." The woman set plates of steaming spaghetti in front of them along with a huge bowl of salad and a basket of fragrant bread. Then offered them bibs, which Rain took for Victoria and for herself.

Rain watched Jack studying his food, and she knew he had too much on his mind. "Relax and eat," she said, spinning some spaghetti around the fork she had pressed into her spoon.

He exhaled, lifted his fork, but didn't start eating.

"Okay," she said. "I know what you're thinking. This isn't up to your standards, not fancy enough or pricey enough, so try to think of it as pasta with flair."

She expected him to set his jaw, mutter something about reading his mind, then ignore the food. But instead, he actually smiled, an expression that stunned her, and began eating. The man had a dimple in his left cheek. She'd never suspected it was there before, and the smile softened his eyes. As much as he angered her with his condescension and snobbery, the smile melted her completely and she was very glad she'd insisted that he come in and have dinner with them.

Chapter Ten

The phone didn't ring for the remainder of the meal and they ate their dinner in peace. By the time they were ready to leave, she felt downright mellow, partly because Jack seemed to be making an effort to talk to Victoria, and partly because she drank more than one glass of wine. They were in the car heading for the loft when she sighed.

"What was that for?" Jack asked, looking at her over Victoria who sat between them again.

"Good food, good wine."

He was watching her through the low light in the car, his eyes narrowed and shadowed. "Yes, very good," he said.

His phone rang and he answered it. "Yes?"

He was listening intently, then he closed his eyes and said, "That sounds like a good idea. I agree to go for it."

He flipped the phone shut, put it in his pocket and the tension that had seemed to disappear, was there again, full-force.

"Bad news?" she asked.

"No, just…" He was the one to sigh heavily this

time. "Things to do." He looked down at Victoria and the little girl was sound asleep, leaning back in the seat, her eyes closed. "Great, the nanny's supposed to be around tonight," he said in a lower voice. "Maybe I can cancel and just ask her to come tomorrow morning instead."

It startled Rain that the idea of not seeing Victoria on a day-to-day basis could make her feel so sad. But she had to get to the hospital soon, so this break was for the best. "I was going to tell you that something happened today that I think is hopeful."

He studied her. "What?"

She told him about Victoria holding up the five fingers earlier. "And she was interested in what the other kids were doing, not just sitting there isolating herself. I think she's trying hard to adjust."

"I hope so," he said and took out his cell phone. "I'll call the nanny to cancel once we're inside," he said as they approached the loft.

Once the car stopped and Jack got out, he handed Rain the keys to his loft. Then he carefully picked up the sleeping child. "Can you bring my briefcase, too?" he asked in a low voice.

"Of course," she said, touched at the paternal gesture toward the child. But before Rain could follow him through the metal security door, someone called out behind them.

"Excuse me? Hello! Excuse me?"

Rain stopped and turned to see a lady hurrying up the sidewalk toward them. She was thin, in a dark dress and low heels. Her short cap of brown hair looked almost mannish. She got close and said, "I'm sorry to bother you, but I have an appointment here, and I've been ringing with no answer for the last ten minutes.''

"Mrs. Willis?'' Rain asked.

The lady was approximately fifty, with a narrow face that seemed washed out in the glow from the security lights that lined the front of the converted warehouse. "Yes, Jane Willis.''

"Mr. Ford's been expecting you,'' she said in a low voice so as not to awaken the child. She motioned to Jack who stood by the elevator cage.

"He was going to call and try to reschedule,'' Rain said. "Victoria fell asleep.''

"I can see that,'' the woman said without hushing her tones at all as she went past Rain to get closer to Jack. "And this was a wasted trip for me.'' She checked her watch. "Just a waste.''

Rain came up beside the woman and watched Jack. She hadn't known him all that long, but she didn't miss the way his jaw set and his eyes narrowed on the woman. "I guess it is,'' he murmured.

"Well, we'll just have to start tomorrow without any orientation.'' She adjusted the strap of her bag on her shoulder. "I don't see how that can be helped. We don't have any other option, short of waking her.''

"Well, we're not waking her,'' Jack said, "But we do have another option.''

"We do?''

"I do. I don't think I'm going to be needing a nanny after all. I've made arrangements that are working out quite well. We'll just forget about tomorrow.'' He looked at Rain. "Can you get the elevator?''

She moved to the cage, lifted the door and heard

Jane Willis. "This is not acceptable. I came all this way because you made an appointment with me."

Jack stepped into the elevator as soon as Rain had the cage door up, and turned to the woman. "You're right," he agreed easily. "I'll contact your employer tomorrow and see that you're compensated for this inconvenience."

She shook her head, but didn't say anything else except, "Great," then left, brushing past Rain. The outer door clanged shut, and Rain stepped into the elevator, tugged down the cage front and pushed the button for the second floor.

"She might have been nice," Rain said in a low voice.

"Might have been, but probably was a direct descendent of Attila the Hun."

Rain laughed softly, then looked at Jack who wasn't laughing at all. "You have no nanny, in case you didn't notice."

He held Victoria, cradling her to him, and she trustingly snuggled into him. "I noticed," he said on a rough sigh. "And I'll get Rita to look again. But my time here is almost over and the current arrangements have been working just fine."

She looked at him, the low-wattage light adding shadows to his features, softening them and making him seem more… She hesitated, trying to find the right word. It was probably better that she didn't and that the elevator stopped right then. She moved to lift the cage door, and hurried to Jack's loft to unlock the door.

She went inside, crossed to the sleeping alcove by the freestanding screen and tugged back the blankets on the small roll-away bed. Standing aside while Jack gently put the little girl on the bed, she then watched him stretch and flex his muscles. "I guess she can sleep in her clothes this once, can't she?" he asked in a whisper.

"I don't see why not," she said. "But maybe you want to take her shoes off?"

He did that, then tugged the blankets over her, took one last look at the little girl and went with Rain into the main area. The only light in the cavernous room came from a single lamp on the side table by the entry, and the filtered glow from an almost full moon that drifted in through the high windows along the back wall. He stopped, faced Rain and said, "About the nanny…"

"You did what you thought was best," she said in a low voice.

"I acted impulsively. The words were out and the deed was done before I realized what it meant."

"As you said, the current arrangement is working out," she agreed, secretly happy that Victoria would be coming to the center tomorrow. "Besides, as you said, you won't be here much longer." He was leaving soon, this week, next week. Soon. "And you're doing okay with her."

"Because of you," he said, his voice even lower. "I really want to thank you for everything you've done." He took a breath. "You're definitely not what I expected."

"You aren't what I expected, either," she said with a slight smile. "Meeting Lizard and not batting an eye, then eating spaghetti as if you enjoyed it."

"I admit to being a bit taken aback by someone

called Lizard, and the spaghetti was fine. Why wouldn't I like it?''

She shrugged. ''I just thought that spaghetti was…well, now don't get mad, but beneath you. That you'd never eat it.''

''But you ordered it….'' He paused, then smiled a shadowy smile. ''Oh, sure, of course, you ordered it for a reason, to make a statement, didn't you? And be honest.''

She couldn't deny that she'd felt a degree of pleasure thinking of him looking at a plate of spaghetti and meatballs and cringing. ''Okay, you got me.''

''This is where I admit that I expected you to order something weird, like green tea noodles in herbal sauce with goat cheese.''

She laughed at that, putting her hand over her mouth to keep the sound as low as possible, then took a breath. ''Oh, you are such a—''

''A snob?'' he asked.

''No, no,'' she murmured, suddenly very aware of the soft intimacy of their conversation, the easy banter that had never been there before. ''Not a snob,'' she whispered.

''Then what?'' he asked, a bit closer.

''I don't know,'' she admitted softly. ''You confuse me. Just when I think I've got you pegged, you…you eat spaghetti and put a child to bed.''

''So, you think you have me pegged?''

''I did.''

''And now?'' he asked in a rough whisper as he touched her. Just the tips of his fingers on her chin, bringing an intense heat with the contact, yet it was a featherlight connection.

She touched her tongue to her lips, her awareness of him so strong that it literally rooted her to the spot. "I don't know," she breathed. He was closer now, so close that she felt his body heat seeping into her. All rational thought was shattered in that moment.

His hand moved, feathering along her jaw line, until his hand cupped her nape under her hair. One contact, yet it was everything. "You don't know what?" he asked, his warm breath fanning across her face.

She didn't know anything about him, except that when he touched her, nothing else mattered. Nothing. And when he slowly lowered his head to kiss her, when she felt his lips on hers, his tongue teasing her, invading her, that was all that existed in the world. The two of them, and this moment.

The kiss went from tentative to intense in the single beat of her heart, flaring into a white-hot passion that flowed through her. Circling his waist with her arms felt like the most natural thing and she pressed her body against the length of his, feeling his desire for her hard against her stomach. His hands moved down her back, cupping her bottom, lifting her up and into him.

The next thing she knew they were on the couch, her under him, him over her, never stopping the kiss, never stopping the connection. His hand came around to her stomach, finding its way under her shirt, against her skin. Searing her, going higher, then managing to push her bra up and releasing her breasts. Her nipple ached when he found it, and she moaned softly, arching toward him. The need to be closer than was humanly possible, consumed her. And she never wanted it to stop.

JACK COULDN'T FIGURE OUT what was happening to him.

Oh, he knew what he was doing…touching, kissing, stroking Rain, and being more involved in it than he was with his own breathing at that moment. But he didn't know how things had gotten to this point. They'd eaten dinner, come back up here, fired a nanny and put a child to bed, then suddenly he'd had to touch her and he did. He'd needed that connection and he'd made it. Now he couldn't stop it.

It was the *why* that ate at him. Why he needed this. Why he couldn't stop. Why he didn't want to stop. Why he wanted more of her than this, more completeness with her, and why his sole thought was of having her. Completely. All to himself. Just him and Rain. Lost together. She moaned and he felt his response to her increase to a deep, terrible ache needing release. He tasted her throat, pulling back her shirt, touching the silky heat of her skin, then finding her breast with his lips.

She jerked sharply, taking a gasp of air, arching toward him, and whatever reason he possessed was gone. Any caution that he'd had moments earlier was shattered. He was feeling her heat, tasting her skin, sensing her need for him rise as quickly as a shooting star. He felt her hands on his stomach, and it startled him that his shirt was gone. No, just unbuttoned. He didn't remember her doing that. Then her hand splayed on his chest, over his heart, and then lower, to his stomach and the tension increased.

From out of nowhere a shrill sound cut through everything, and he felt Rain go still under him. The connection was gone. He pushed back, barely able to endure the sight of her under him, her face flushed, her lips softly parted, her chest rising and falling rapidly, her rosy nipples hard nubs. And it took all his willpower to push farther away and off her.

The phone. That was the noise. He took a deep breath meant to steady him, but it came more as a shudder and he turned from Rain, raking his fingers through his hair as he stood to distance himself.

He reached for the nearest phone quickly, and as he gripped the receiver and cut off the rings, he was stunned to realize that he'd totally forgotten that Victoria was there, just feet away from them. Behind the screen. "Hello?" he growled after clearing his throat.

"Jack, love, it's me," Eve said. "I was hoping you'd be there."

Eve. Reality crushed him. Damn it. "Eve, is something wrong?" he asked.

"What could be wrong, love? I'm sitting on the balcony of this fabulous villa, the breeze coming in off the ocean. The only thing wrong is that you're not here." She laughed, a throaty laugh. "I wish you were. They're having a party, lots of fun. It's perfect, except you're in Houston."

He closed his eyes tightly, focusing and feeling his body begin to adjust, the ache subsiding. He heard movement behind him, Rain stirring, but he didn't turn. He kept his eyes closed. "As long as you're having fun."

"Oh, I am, yes, I am, most certainly." She paused, then said, as if she'd just remembered, "I'm still so sorry that I couldn't see you when the plane landed, but the connecting flight was all messed up."

"I'd been hoping you could have stayed for a few

days,'' he said, a bit unnerved that the completion of that sentence in his mind was, ''To help me make sense out of everything.''

''Me, too. But soon, when your business gets settled, then we'll celebrate.''

''Absolutely. I hope I can get things tied up soon, then…'' His voice trailed off. Then what? Tell her that he'd acted like a fool with another woman, that the man who prized loyalty as much as honesty above all else was verging on being not only disloyal, but dishonest, too. He hated that. ''We'll be together soon.''

''How's Victoria? Did you get a nanny okay?''

''She's okay.''

''You know, love, someone at the party was saying that you should find a really good child psychologist. That maybe she needs help with not talking and all.''

He'd found one, a very good one, and he was almost thinking that he needed one for himself. ''That sounds like a good idea. We'll talk about it later.''

There were voices in the background, laughter and loud music. ''Oh, my, they're moving the party down to the pool,'' Eve said, trying to be heard over the noise. ''I need to go.'' She laughed, then said, ''Call me soon?''

''Of course I will.''

''I love you, Jack.''

''Love you,'' he murmured.

The line clicked and she was gone.

Jack took a breath, then opened his eyes, put the phone down and braced himself to face Rain, to try to figure out how to explain what had just happened. But he turned to find an empty loft. She was gone.

MEDITATION. HERB TEA. More mediation. Centering. Focusing. More herb tea. None of it worked, and finally, Rain made a phone call.

"It's me," Rain said, not at all surprised that her mother was wide-awake at midnight. Bree worked when she wanted to work. She wasn't a painter like George, but a writer, and when the spirit moved her, she wrote.

"Rainbow, honey, I'm so glad you called," she said in her soft voice, the voice that brought immediate peace with it. Except tonight. "What's wrong, is it the hospital position?"

"They still can't hire, and I'm in limbo."

"Is that what's wrong?"

"Not just that," she said, shocked at the sting of hot tears behind her eyes. She wasn't a crier, she never had been, but she was very close to crying at that moment. "I just don't know what I'm going to do."

"Well, Rainbow, you can always come on back here. I'd love that, and you could do whatever you want out here."

"I know," she said softly. "I just…"

"Baby, your father told me that you're stressed, that he's worried about you."

She almost laughed at that. When he'd been here her biggest stress had been the job. Jack and Victoria hadn't factored into it. "Anyone's stressed next to George," she said with a shaky laugh.

"Well, I can't argue with that," Bree murmured.

There was a muffled noise coming from somewhere, and it almost sounded like a scream, then it was gone. "Rainbow? Are you still there?"

"Yes, I am, I...I need to go, though," she said, listening, but didn't hear the noise again.

"Rainbow. Listen to me. Don't let the bureaucracy at the hospital upset you. I know you're doing this because you want to help, and that's a wonderful thing, but there are other ways to give back to humanity. Don't let them wear you down."

A grand concept, but it had nothing to do with how she felt just now. "I won't."

"Good. Love and peace," Bree said, then was gone.

Rain hung up and had barely set the phone back on its base when a sudden pounding on the door startled her. It came again, and she hurried over to the door. "Who is it?" she called out.

"Jack."

God, that was all she needed. Jack. She'd spent hours castigating herself for what she'd done, hours of trying to make reason out of chaos, and hours of feeling empty, the echo of his voice saying, "Love you," to Eve over the phone still ringing in her ears. Now he was here.

"What do you want?"

Jack's response was muffled, but she could have sworn he said, "Help," but there was another noise, a horribly sad noise, of someone crying. Quickly, she undid the lock and looked out into the corridor. Not only was Jack there wearing just pajama bottoms, but in his arms was Victoria. The child was sobbing uncontrollably, her face buried in his shoulder, her arms clutching him around his neck.

"What's going on?" she asked.

At the sound of her voice, the little girl twisted

toward her, holding out her arms and all but leaping into Rain's embrace. She caught her and pulled her to her. Her small body was shaking and she was gasping, as if she couldn't breathe. Her little face was beet red, stained with tears. "What is it, sweetie? A bad dream?"

"I don't know what it is," Jack said, "but she just started screaming, and I found her ripping the bed apart. I thought it was the cat, but he took off right away. When I tried to get her to stop, she bolted for the door. If it hadn't been locked she would have been out before I could catch her. I think she was coming over here."

She held Victoria tightly, rocking her, talking softly. "Sweetie, it's okay. Whatever's wrong, we'll fix it. But you have to tell me what it is." The little girl moved back a bit in her arms, looking at her, the pain in her eyes unbearable. "A bad dream?" Rain asked.

The shake of her head, was so sharp that it shocked Rain.

"Okay, not a bad dream. You want something?"

An emphatic yes nod of her head.

"You…lost something?"

She nodded fervently.

Oh, she knew what it was. She could almost visualize the restaurant, the doll sitting in the extra chair and them leaving. The doll had been left at the restaurant. "Your doll, we left her, didn't we?"

Her eyes got large and she nodded vigorously.

Rain looked at Jack. "It's the doll. We have to get it back."

"At two in the morning?"

"We have to try." She turned and went into the loft, heading for the phone. She dropped down on a bunch of pillows, holding Victoria on her lap. She passed the phone book to Jack. "Get the number."

"They won't be open."

"Lizard lives there. He'll answer if you let it ring long enough."

Jack took the book, flipped to the yellow pages, then found it. He just hoped that Lizard was home. It rang six times before someone picked up. "Hello?"

"Lizard?"

"Yeah, man," he said, obviously not annoyed at being roused at two in the morning.

"This is Jack Ford. I was there tonight—"

"With Rainbow. Yeah, what can I do for you?"

"Victoria left her doll there at the table. I was wondering if you found it."

"Sure did, Jack. A well-worn rag doll?"

"That's the one."

He put his hand over the mouthpiece. "He has it," he said, then spoke to Lizard again. "Is there any way I can come and get it now?"

The man didn't hesitate. "Sure, man, but you caught me on my way out. I'm heading to the airport."

"Can you leave it somewhere, then, or with someone?"

"Forget that. Why don't I just drop it by on my way?"

"Could you?"

"No problem."

Jack gave him the address, told him to ring either Rain's loft or his, then hung up.

Chapter Eleven

The voice was tiny, barely audible, but the name was clear. Jack looked at Rain and saw the same disbelief in her eyes that he felt. "Emma?" he asked softly. "That's your doll's name?"

Victoria turned her face into Rain's shoulder, but nodded.

"You named her?" he asked.

She nodded again.

"That's a beautiful name," he murmured around a lump in his throat.

"So, she's Emma," Rain said softly, staring at Jack while she held the child and he thought he saw the sheen of tears in Rain's brown eyes. "Do you think Emma would like it if we got her new clothes to let her know how happy we are that she's safe?" Rain asked the child, never taking her eyes off Jack.

Victoria shifted on Rain's lap, and sat back a bit to look up at her. Jack expected another nod again, but instead, she spoke again, one simple word. "Yes." Her voice was tiny, little more then a whispery thread of sound, but so very real.

"And how about we get you clothes to match Emma's and then you can be twins?" Rain asked.

The little girl nodded, and cuddled into Rain's hold again. Jack saw Rain swallow hard and again noticed the tears in her eyes, and that her lashes were damp. "I totally forgot about the doll," she said to him in a slightly unsteady voice.

"You aren't the only one," he said, as a tear slipped down her cheek.

He reached out and brushed at the single tear with the tip of his fingers. He felt her tremble slightly, and as much as he'd wanted to kiss her earlier in the evening, now he just wanted to hold her. He drew back, then stood. "Does anyone want anything?" he asked, not willing to think about what he wanted. He was crazy. "Milk, juice, tea?"

Victoria nodded yes.

He didn't want to push her, but decided that he'd try to just ask. "Which one? Milk, or juice?"

He saw her take a small breath, then reply, "Milk."

He looked at Rain again, and wished he hadn't. She'd caught her hair in a single braid that fell down her back, wore another version of her tie-dyed T-shirts and didn't have a speck of makeup on. She looked painfully beautiful. Her eyes were still overly bright from the barely contained tears, her lips softly parted, and her lashes damply spiked. He was out of control. He knew it. He just didn't know what to do about it. "Do…do you want something?"

"No…thanks," she said in a voice so low he could barely hear her.

He turned from the sight of her holding Victoria,

and he headed to his loft. When he came back with a small glass of milk for Victoria, she and Rain were lying in the pile of pillows, cuddled together. He put the milk on a low table near them, looked for a chair, but finally just sat on the floor.

He felt as if his world had shifted again, the same way it had years ago. When his father had died. When he'd found out what Clayton had done to Robert and LynTech. When he'd hired on at LynTech. When he'd taken over their European office. Ian and Jean's deaths. Victoria. Then coming here. He watched Rain help Victoria get the milk and it hit him that he hadn't thought about Eve. Meeting her and deciding to get married should have been on that list.

Before he could analyze what everything meant the buzzer sounded. He went to the call box and pushed the button. "Yes?"

"It's Lizard, and I have a doll with me."

He buzzed him in.

In less then a minute, Lizard appeared wearing a tie-dyed shirt, cut off jeans and rope sandals. "I can't tell you how much we appreciate this," Jack said, meeting the man in the corridor. "Can I repay you somehow?"

Lizard smiled. "Absolutely. Let me see your two beautiful ladies."

Jack nodded. "Of course. Victoria's going to want to thank you for bringing Emma back."

The two men went into the loft and Lizard crossed to where Victoria and Rain sat in the pillows. He hunkered down in front of them and held the doll out to the child. "She's been real good, very polite and well behaved. I even put her in a seat belt on the way over here. I told her Victoria was waiting for her.''

Victoria reached for Emma, hugged her to her chest and grinned at Lizard, an expression of pure happiness. ''Thank you,'' she said softly.

''Oh, you're very welcome,'' Lizard said as he stood and looked at his watch. ''I've gotta go.''

''Thanks so much, Lizard,'' Rain said.

''Forget it. All's well and all that stuff,'' he said with a smile and glanced around. ''Who would have thought that George did these?'' He moved closer to the red one. ''A real mind-blower.'' He looked at Rain. ''What is it, therapy?''

''Lifelong therapy,'' Rain said.

''Who'd know he ever did my piece.'' Lizard shook his head. ''No waves and surf in this stuff,'' he said.

Jack realized he was talking about the painting at the restaurant. The Hawaiian seascape, so intricately beautiful that he'd felt as though he could step right into it. ''George painted the canvas in your entry?''

''Sure did. It's a genuine Dune.'' He grinned. ''Damn, never thought I'd get one of those. But one day he just came by and gave it to me.'' He shook his head. ''Hell, I know what a Dune sells for. I was shocked, but I didn't refuse.''

Jack shook his head. ''I never expected…''

''Me, neither,'' the man said, then continued, ''I'm out of here, and best wishes to all of you in everything you do.''

''Same to you, Lizard,'' Rain murmured.

''I'll walk you out,'' Jack said and went with him

out of the loft and to the elevator, lifting the front of the cage to let him get in.

"No reason to go down with me, man," Lizard said as he stepped into the car. "Go back to your ladies."

Jack didn't argue. He tugged down the front of the cage, then nodded to Lizard. "Thanks again."

The man gave him a partial salute as the elevator started down. "Peace and love," he said, then he was gone.

Jack went back into Rain's loft, and as he crossed to where she and Victoria were, he saw that they both had their eyes closed. They were snuggled down into the pillows, Victoria hugging the doll and Rain hugging her. His ladies? He was letting things get totally out of control and he couldn't afford that. He crouched, touching Rain on her foot.

Her eyes fluttered open and she looked at him. "Emma," she said softly.

He knew right then, if he'd been looking for love, he would have found it right here. But he wasn't looking, and this didn't make sense. Love? He didn't even know what that was. He thought he loved Eve. He was going to marry her. But whatever he felt for Eve was nothing like the feelings Rain stirred in him. He drew his hand back, afraid to touch her again. "She can talk," he breathed.

"Oh, yes, she sure can," Rain said in a whisper.

Rain was trying very hard to ignore Jack, to ignore the fact that he was half-dressed and she was half-dressed and it was the middle of the night and his voice was very soft. She found herself almost not breathing as she lay in the pillows holding the child.

She'd never acted so foolishly or so irrationally in all
her life as she had earlier. She'd never lost her head
with a man. She'd never come close to doing something she knew was so wrong, for both of them.

Thank God Eve had called right then, that she'd
heard Jack say he loved Eve. And that she'd silently
left the apartment before he knew she was gone. She
didn't know what would have happened if she had
stayed. At least she'd done the smart thing and left.

And she was going to do the smart thing again. She
eased back from the child, then managed to push up
and stand. She looked down at Victoria as she slept.
Yes, this was the smartest thing for everyone. "She
needs to go back to bed with Emma this time," she
said and stood back to let Jack pick up the child. He
cradled her in his arms and turned to Rain. Silently,
she went ahead of him into his loft, over to the roll-
away bed, and she saw the evidence of the terror the
child had shown when she woke without her doll.

Blankets had been torn off the bed, and the mattress
was skittered sideways on the springs. She quickly
remade the bed, then stood back and let Jack put Victoria down. The child cuddled into the sheets with her
doll as Jack covered her. Then he turned and looked
at Rain. That was all it took for her to move, to make
her escape. A smart thing, considering all she really
wanted was to walk into his arms.

But his arms weren't open, and she didn't have the
right to even think that. She headed for the door, and
touched the handle right when his voice stopped her.

"Rain?"

She turned partly, but never let go of the door handle. "Yes?"

"We need to talk."

"No, we don't," Rain said.

"Yes, we do," he countered and went toward her.

She stayed at the door, her hand clutching the handle tightly. "Okay, let me make this easy for both of us. Whatever happened tonight, shouldn't have happened. Period."

She saw him take a deep breath, as if to steady himself, and she wished with all her heart that he was dressed, and not standing there in the pajama bottoms that rode low on his hips. She didn't want to see him like that and she didn't want to see the "T" that the hair on his chest formed, the width of his shoulders, or the sleek tanned skin.

"You're right," he said in a low voice. "I'm sorry. Things have been crazy, and you've done such a great job with Victoria. I don't know how to thank you or how to pay you back."

Her stomach clenched. "A simple thank-you is just fine," she murmured.

There was a long silence, then he said, "Are you going to be at the center tomorrow?"

She almost said, "No," but couldn't. "I should be."

"Good, good," he said softly.

She nodded, her hand aching from its grip on the door handle. His phone rang and he just stood there staring at her. On the fourth ring, she said, "Aren't you going to answer it?"

He silently crossed to it, and lifted the receiver. "Yes?"

He listened, not speaking, then he said one word. "Eve."

Rain turned and left, closing the door behind her, just as she'd done a few hours ago. But this time she knew that the most foolish thing she'd ever done in her life didn't amount to a hill of beans next to the fact that she was very close to falling in love with Jack Ford.

BETWEEN THE PLANS for the charity ball and the business crisis at LynTech, the next day didn't go the way Rain expected it to. She braced herself to see Jack again and to push away whatever feelings she had for him. But he never showed up at the center. Rita brought Victoria down first thing in the morning, and that was that.

During the day Victoria started to open up, actually getting involved in a game some kids were playing by the fake tree, and saying a few words to them. When Mary passed out cookies midmorning, Victoria looked up, took a cookie and said softly, "Thank you."

Mary blinked rapidly, then said, "You're most welcome," gave Victoria the last two cookies, and hurried back to the office.

Rain saw that Victoria was fine with the other kids, then said, "I'll be right back," and followed the older woman. When she stepped into the office, Mary was by the desk, wiping her eyes with a Kleenex.

"Now, if that isn't a miracle," the woman said, balling the tissue up in her hands as she sank down in the chair behind the desk. "Just a miracle, a real miracle." She smiled at Rain. "And you did it."

"No, no, I didn't," she said, and told Mary about the incident with the doll. "She's ready to start healing and she's crazy about...Mr. Ford. I think they'll be fine.''

''Oh, my, this is such a great day,'' Mary said with a sigh, then looked at Rain, her gaze skimming over her jeans and loose white shirt. ''So, how about you?''

''Me?'' she asked, stunned for a minute thinking that the woman had read her mind and knew about the mess she'd made in her own life. ''What about me?''

''Your job? Have you heard anything?''

She released a breath, relieved. ''Oh, my job. No, I called yesterday and it's still hung up with the budget committee.''

''Bureaucracy,'' Mary said with a frown. ''That's what I've always hated about big business.'' She sighed. ''That and the arrogance that goes with the power. The single-mindedness you have to have in order to be a success.''

''You sound like my father. But he calls it bureaucratic garbage.''

''All boils down to the same thing,'' Mary murmured. ''Never understood it, never could.''

''Me, neither,'' Rain said.

''Take Mr. Ford for example,'' she said.

''What about Mr. Ford?''

''Seems like a very nice man.''

''He is.''

''And he seems sort of...'' She shrugged. ''I don't know, lost, maybe?''

That was one word that Rain would never have applied to Jack. ''Lost? How?''

''In his life. I get the sense that he's a fixer. Stress-

He'd been on the fire escape landing trying to sort through his life when Victoria had first screamed, shattering the night and making his heart race. When he'd found her his first thought once he'd managed to pick her up was to get over here to Rain. He'd known she'd understand the child's terror, and she had. He hadn't even thought of the doll.

He crouched in front of Victoria while she clung to Rain, but her huge eyes were on him. "Your doll's fine and Lizard said he's bringing her home." He looked at Rain. "He offered."

Victoria let out a breath and seemed to almost collapse against Rain. "Isn't that great, sweetie?" Rain said, brushing a kiss across the child's forehead. "Your doll's safe. So, we'll wait and when Lizard gets here, you'll have…whatever her name is, back."

Victoria swallowed hard, and said very clearly, "Emma."

ing over this business mess and over the little girl and over…whatever he can find to stress over." She shrugged again. "I could see that he was uneasy with what he thought you were."

She did more than read minds. She looked into people's souls. "Oh, you could?"

"It was pretty obvious, the free spirit, and the…" She shrugged again. "Whatever. But I'll bet that now he sees you in a different light."

She saw him in a different light, as well, out from under the blanket of the corporate monied snob that she'd first thought him to be. "I don't know if he does or not," she admitted.

"Oh, I think he does. I don't think he'd let you around the child if he really thought badly of you."

Would he kiss me, and touch me? She could feel her legs getting unsteady and it shocked her. Thankfully there was a knock on the door right then, and Mary called out, "Come in."

When the door opened, Rain saw something akin to shock stamped on Mary's face. Rain turned and saw Robert Lewis coming into the office. The man took a single step, then stopped and looked at Mary with the same expression. Shock.

"Mary?" Robert said, then slowly came farther into the office. "You work here? I've been down here every day, to see Brittany or Anthony, and I never saw…" His voice trailed off as Mary stood, the Kleenex systematically being destroyed by her hands worrying it. "I didn't know you were here."

Rain saw Mary smile, a tight version of her usual expression, but she knew that something was wrong. Very wrong. But she couldn't begin to figure out what. "What a lovely surprise," she said, but it didn't sound as if it was lovely at all. Mary looked at Rain. "Robert…Mr. Lewis and I, we used to know each other." She looked at Robert and said in a low voice, "In another lifetime."

"Why didn't you let me know you were working here? I thought you had left Houston years ago."

"I came back," she said, "and I just didn't think that you'd be interested."

His expression tightened just a bit, but his voice stayed conversational. "I think Brittany told me the new assistant was Mary Garner, not Powers."

"Garner's my married name," Mary said, as she came around the desk, keeping Rain between herself and Robert. "And I've met your daughter. Just a lovely woman. And Anthony. A terrific kid," she said, speaking faster than Rain had ever heard her speak before. "And now I need to get back to work."

"Can we talk for a minute?" Robert asked.

Mary stopped beside Rain. "Talk?"

"It's been thirty years."

"I know."

Rain looked from one to the other, then said, "I need to get back to Victoria. She's going to be looking for me."

Robert looked at her. "Oh, I almost forgot. Jack asked me to let you know that he was going to be late tonight. A meeting. He'll be down at six."

"Thanks," she said, then walked out of the office. As she headed toward Victoria who was playing alone with blocks at the foot of the tree, she heard the door to the office close. Ten minutes later, Robert left, not looking left or right, and Mary didn't come out of the office for a very long time. When she did, it was to tell Rain that Dr. Shay was on the phone.

JACK PACED THE FLOOR in his office, paperwork scattered everywhere, and nothing done. Focus, he told himself. Just focus. He looked at the clock. Five-thirty. The meeting had been called off at the last minute, and he'd thought he could take advantage of the extra time before he had to go and get Victoria. He'd been wrong. All he'd done was pace, think and pace some more. And nothing fit. Nothing made sense.

He was a man used to knowing where he was going, knowing what he wanted and why. "Focus, damn it," he muttered to the empty office. "Focus." And he did. He got some papers together to take home, shrugged into his dark-brown suit coat and left the office.

He didn't get very far when he saw Robert leave Matt's office and hurry down the corridor toward him. "Have you see Matt anywhere? He's not in his office, and neither is Rita."

"It's after five, and I think he and Brittany were going to check out the place Sommers offered for the ball. His house, or some hall or something."

They met at the elevators. "Oh, I forgot all about that. It's Sommers's estate. He suddenly offered its use." Robert shook his head. "I guess it's a write-off or something."

Jack didn't understand much of anything E. J. Sommers did. He pushed the call button. "Are you heading down?"

Robert hesitated, then said, "No, no, I don't think

so. I need to get some things out of the conference room.'' He patted Jack on the shoulder. ''You take care of yourself.''

Jack nodded as Robert walked away. When the elevator car arrived, Jack pushed the button for the lobby level. ''Just focus,'' he muttered to himself. This was a blip. He'd be going back to London soon, and life would settle down.

When he reached the lobby Jack headed for the day-care center. That's when he collided with another human being. He felt the impact, but kept his balance and found himself looking down at Rain. She grabbed his arm to keep from falling backward, then steadied herself and looked up.

''Oh, my gosh, I'm sorry, Jack.'' She let him go and he could see that she looked bothered. ''I wasn't watching where I was going. I'm really sorry,'' she said, nervously brushing at his jacket as if she'd mussed it or something.

''What's wrong?'' he asked, not missing the slight shakiness in her hand, or the way her hair was escaping from the single braid, or how pale her skin appeared. ''You look as if someone's chasing you.''

''No one's chasing me.'' She stopped worrying his jacket and brushed at her face, skimming back the errant wisps of hair. ''I just had a terrible afternoon, and I was trying to get back before Victoria left.'' She spoke in a breathy, rushed voice. ''I was worried about leaving her here, but she seemed okay with Mary. She's been talking more today, and actually playing with the other kids.''

''That's good news,'' he said, and resisted the urge to take her hand in his to keep it still.

"Yes, it is," she said and turned to head for the doors, muttering something that he barely caught as he fell in step beside her.

"What was so terrible about the afternoon?" he asked. She reached to push back the door, ignoring what he'd asked, but he stopped her. "What's wrong?"

"Nothing." She sighed. "Everything. The hospital, they aren't sure they'll ever be able to put me on staff. The budget and other things." She shrugged, a fluttery movement that seemed incredibly vulnerable to him. "George always says to go with the flow and let things just happen, and I'm usually pretty good at that." She frowned at him. "Okay, I know you don't like that kind of philosophy, but I realize now that it makes failure a bit easier to deal with."

"I wouldn't call it a failure if they can't find the budget to take you on. Sounds like a business decision, and nothing more."

She tilted her head a bit to one side and looked up at him. "Why am I not surprised that you said that?" she murmured, then waved that away with another sigh. "I'm sorry. That's not fair. It's just your opinion, and probably a whole lot better then mine."

She was apologizing and that bothered him, too. Maybe because it felt as if she was giving up, and that wasn't like her. "What do you do now?"

"I wish I knew," she breathed, and with that, she turned, pushed back the doors and went into the center.

Jack was left standing there, never feeling so alone in all his life.

Chapter Twelve

Jack followed Rain into a space that looked deserted. Then he saw Mary and Victoria off to the right. The older woman and the child sat on the floor, bottles of paint by them, and a long expanse of paper in front of them, maybe twenty feet long and three feet high. "What are you two up to?" he asked, aware of Rain right by his side.

"Oh, Mr. Ford," Mary said, sitting back on her heels and looking up at him and Rain. "My goodness, is it that late already?"

"It's just after six," Jack said. He could see that someone had drawn wonderful pencil sketches depicting a long line of children, holding hands and smiling. Then he looked at what Victoria was doing, patiently coloring in the shoes on a little girl. Victoria was smiling, her face lifted in pleasure. He noticed that the picture she was working on resembled her, down to and including the blond braids. "What is this?" he asked.

"Brittany did the sketches and each child paints and colors themselves. It's a banner to display at the charity ball. Victoria didn't seem to want to do it at first, but now she's really enjoying it. She's doing a wonderful job, don't you think, Mr. Ford?''

"Wonderful," he said as Rain crouched by Victoria.

"This is incredible," she said. "I heard Brittany was doing something for the ball, and I know she's talented. The murals are great. But these... They look just like the children and you, Mary." She pointed to the drawing of Mary holding Victoria's hand. "Oh, my goodness."

"Yes, that's me," Mary said, "And I have to color mine, too. I don't have an artistic bone in my body, but I'm willing to try."

Victoria looked up at Jack and grinned. "It's me, Uncle Jack."

"It certainly is," he said, and noticed that Brittany had even drawn Victoria holding her doll. "I'm impressed," he murmured, happy to see Victoria kneeling on the floor by Mary, painting. A totally normal thing for a four-year-old to do. "It's great, and I'm sorry to break this up, but we need to get going."

He watched as her tiny bottom lip jutted out just a bit and she frowned. She was pouting? "Can I just color me?" she asked.

Now that she was speaking in that soft, clear voice, he couldn't believe this was the same child who had landed on his door step such a short time ago. "You can finish tomorrow, can't she?" he asked Mary.

"Well, to be perfectly honest—and I do believe we should be honest with the children—no she can't do it tomorrow. It's Saturday, and even though we have a session tomorrow, it's a session away from here, a field trip. So, in all honesty, we won't be able to do this again until next week, and when we do, the other kids are pretty rowdy and, to be honest, once again, Victoria does better in a one-on-one situation.''

He didn't know whether to laugh or scream. It felt so much like Mrs. Ferris giving him a rundown on Victoria's activities. "Then she can't do it next week?''

"Well, of course, she can," Mary said. "But I'm staying here for a while to work on my portrait, and if Victoria wants to, she can stay with me, and we can work together. Of course, it's up to you.''

Jack hadn't realized, until then, how everything he did revolved around Victoria. Every moment away from work was geared to make sure she was okay. "I don't know if—''

Victoria touched Jack on the pant leg. "Can I please stay?''

"I guess it's okay. I can do some more work and—''

"Oh, goodness, no, Mr. Ford, you run along. I can drive Victoria to your place when we're done.'' She glanced at Rain. "You look a bit peeked, dear. You run along and get some rest. Your meeting with Mr. Shay didn't go well, did it?''

"Not at all. And then I came out and this used car I finally bought wouldn't start, so it was towed to a garage, and I got a taxi back here. If you don't need me, I'll just call another taxi and go home.''

"Taxies are just a terrible way to go," she said, then looked at Jack. "You have a car, don't you?''

"It's waiting outside.''

"You live in the same building. Why not kill two birds with one stone, and ride together?''

He looked at Rain, then asked, "How about it?"

"I think—"

"You know, you both think too much. Believe me, no good comes from it. I know that for a fact. Every time I really thought about what I was going to do, I made mistakes. Just take the ride and get some rest."

Rain looked at Jack, then nodded. "Okay."

"Good, good," Mary said, smiling. "I'll be by around eight with Victoria. I'll give her a bite to eat so you won't have to worry about feeding her."

Jack looked at Rain, and she looked worn-out, almost delicate, and he remembered her calling him a "fixer." At that moment, he wanted to "fix" her. Just to make her smile. "Let's go," he said.

RAIN LEFT WITH JACK, thinking about the sudden turn of events, and what she'd found out earlier this afternoon.

After the meeting at the hospital with Dr. Shay, Rain had felt vaguely lost. "It appears that there might not be the funds needed to implement expanding the staff. But we foresee a turnaround in the future, although not in the immediate future," he'd said. In plain English, she knew that meant that she could stay in Houston, but working at the hospital was probably out of the question. If she stayed here, she had to get another job. Her savings would only keep her going for so long. Or she could go back to the Coast and see about finding a position there.

Now, Jack had her by her arm and was gently urging her toward the door. She barely had time to say goodbye to Victoria and Mary before they'd reached the waiting company car. Jack continued to hold her upper arm and she didn't pull away.

They got into the car, and the driver asked, "Where to, sir?"

Jack hesitated, then looked at Rain. "Are you hungry?"

She thought she was, but had been too tired to even worry about it. "I guess so, but—"

"Okay, this time I pick the place," he said.

"No, you don't have to—"

"No, I don't, but I'm hungry and there isn't much at the loft."

There wasn't much at George's, either, just some tofu, apples and a variety of teas. "Okay."

He turned to the driver. "Can you take us to the Three Coins?"

"Yes, sir," he said and closed the door.

Rain looked at Jack. "Oh, no. Even I know about the Three Coins, not that I've ever been there, but I do know that a single potato there would cost enough to ravage my savings. And I'm not dressed for a place like that."

"I'm paying."

"Oh, no you're not."

"Of course I am. I'm choosing, so I'm paying."

"I chose Our Place, and I didn't pay there."

"And you never even fought me over the check," he said, the shadow of a smile playing at the corners of his mouth.

"That's different."

"No, it's not."

"I'm not dressed for a nice place," she repeated. Jeans and a loose shirt weren't what you wore to a

place like the Three Coins, or to an appointment with
the doctor who held your future in his hands, either.
She wasn't going to make another mistake. "I mean,
jeans and a shirt?"

He flicked his gaze over her. "You're fine."

"I am not," she said.

"Listen, I know you hate big money, but one thing
you need to know is, if you have enough money, you
can go into a place like this in your bed slippers and
bathrobe and I guarantee someone will say, with great
sincerity, 'My, don't you look absolutely lovely this
evening,' and they'll make you believe it."

"I look like a kitchen worker," she muttered, angry at herself that she suddenly wished she was in a
lovely dress and had makeup on, and three-inch heels.

"You look…" His voice trailed off, then he said
softly, "You look absolutely lovely this evening."

"Now, that's an exaggeration," she said.

"Do I have to point out that I went to your place
and met a man named Lizard when you wanted to?"

"Kicking and screaming."

"Another exaggeration," he said. "I went. I ate. I
didn't complain, and I never mentioned the man's
name."

"You wouldn't put on a bib."

"And I won't make you wear a bib at the Three
Coins, either."

She sank back in the leather, fighting a smile. "I
bet they only speak French there."

"I'll order for both of us."

She cast him a sideways glance. "You speak
French?"

"Some."

"And Japanese?"

"Enough."

"Any other languages?"

"German, Spanish and touch of Italian, but that's not my strong suit."

"I take it you went to a lot of boarding schools when you were growing up?"

"I went to two, both in this country. But I do have a way with languages, and when I went overseas to head the operations there, it seemed sensible to be able to speak directly to our business associates."

"I'm impressed," she said.

"Don't be," he said with a smile that made her feel slightly weak. And that dimple. Even in the interior lights, she could see it. "I can't carry a tune to save my life."

It was her turn to finally smile. Before long they were in a very expensive area of the city, an area she had been to very seldom. They came to a stop at the stone portico entry to the Three Coins. A line of cars were waiting for the valet, cars that cost more than she'd make in years.

Jack got out, turned and held his hand out to her.

"We're here," he murmured.

That they were, and she felt even more awkward than she thought she would. She didn't belong here, but Jack was acting as if she did. She hesitated, then she looked right at him, at that confidence in his expression and his hand held out to her. If he could make this work, so could she. She put her hand in his, felt his fingers close around hers and she got out into the night.

The Three Coins was like an elegant manor house

inside, with private side rooms and a huge ballroom-like central area. But Jack had been right. In the midst of deep reds, gilt trims, heavy wooden floors and plush carpeting, no one looked at her twice. No one raised an eyebrow or looked shocked at her appearance. They were shown to a room with a view of the city rolling off into the distance. A white grand piano sat on a platform, while a man played tunes from the forties.

She was so far out of her comfort zone, that she actually was starting to see this as one big joke. The daughter of George Armstrong in a place like this, with people like this. It was a joke. She brushed at her hair, nervously trying to tuck an errant strand behind her ears. She couldn't pretend to belong here, and despite her protestation about paying her own way, she knew she wouldn't. She couldn't. But Jack could.

Jack ordered in French, then as the waiter left and the pianist started playing an old Cole Porter song, Jack said, "I hope you like salmon."

"Yes, yes, I do."

"Good," he said. "Do me a favor?"

"What?"

"Stop fussing with your hair and have a drink."

She put her hands on the table by the place setting that consisted of layers of plates, and rows of utensils. She stared at the three goblets in front of her, one she was sure contained water and a wafer thin lemon wedge. The other had a light liquid and the third was empty. She had no idea what the waiter had poured into the second one. "I'm fine."

Jack reached toward her, his right hand covering

her left. "No, you're not and I'm sorry. I thought this was a good idea."

Rain looked at him, shocked at the tenderness in his tone and his touch, and just as shocked that it made tears prick at the backs of her eyes. "It's not your fault," she managed to reply around a heavy lump in her throat.

"Yes, it is. I thought this would be nice after the day you had, and that we could talk and I could make up for all that brandy I drank." His hand tightened slightly on hers. "Bad idea?"

A kind idea. A nice idea. But a bad idea. "I'm sorry," she whispered.

"No, don't be," he said and stood, coming around to her. And he held out his hand to her again. "Come on. Let's go."

She looked around. "You can't just leave after you ordered," she said.

"Of course I can," he said, and she thought that he probably could do anything he wanted.

She took his hand and stood, then he walked with her out into the greeting area, and said, "Stay here," while he went to talk to a man in a tux. She heard Jack say, "I'm sorry, we have to leave." He took out his wallet. "I do hope this covers it."

Rain saw the man take some bills from Jack, then smile. "But of course, sir."

Jack returned, slipped his arm around her shoulders as if it were the most natural thing in the world, and they left. The driver was there with the car and they were back in it in no time. Rain sat stiffly on the leather seat, staring straight ahead.

Neither of them spoke for what seemed a very long

time. Then she finally made herself say, "I appreciate what you tried to do, but it was a bad idea."

"I can see that it was," he murmured.

She looked at him, and asked, "Then why did you do it?"

He shrugged. "I don't know. I thought..." He let his words trail off. "I was wrong."

He sure was, and so was she. She brushed at her eyes, hating the feeling of dampness there. Damn it, she wasn't a crier, never had been. But around him it was becoming a habit. Especially when she thought about Eve Ryder, and how she would fit into that place. Perfectly.

When Jack touched her hand as it curled into a fist on her thigh, she froze. "It isn't worth crying over, is it?"

"I'm not crying," she lied.

He laughed at that, a rough, deep sound that ran across her frayed nerves. "Sure you aren't. And pigs fly."

She jerked away from him, brushing at her face again. "What do you want from me?"

He stared at her, his dark eyes narrowed and intense. Then she heard him exhale. "Oh, boy, you shouldn't ask that."

She felt her breath catch in her chest when he lifted his hand, brushing at her cheek with the tips of his fingers. Then his index finger traced the line of her jaw, from her ear to chin, then slowly lifted to touch her full bottom lip. "Jack?" she whispered.

"Shhh." He moved closer and drew her to him, cradling her to his chest, and she curled into it. She drank in the feeling of his arms around her, of his heart beating against her cheek. She felt him surround her and his essence invade her. And she knew a sense of belonging that she'd never experienced before in her life. A sense of being in a place that was so right, so perfect, that she literally was afraid to breathe or move in case it all dissolved.

But Jack did move. He held her back a bit, looked down at her, and she understood so much at that moment. Love? She thought so. She'd never been in love, so she didn't really know, but it felt like what love should. His touch, his closeness. She wanted him to never let go. That felt like love. Then he kissed her, a soft kiss, a reassuring kiss. His taste was on her lips, and she seemed to be inhaling his essence. She blinked, stunned. Love. Yes, love.

Then she felt him move away as the car slowed to a stop. His fingers brushed her cheek one last time, and that was it. Suddenly she felt very alone. She looked away from Jack and reached for her bag, anything to keep from reaching for him again. No, this couldn't be. But what if she wanted it and Jack wanted it? She felt a rise of something akin to hope, pushing aside all the rational reasons that told her this was insanity.

Jack touched her again, his hand on her arm. "We're here," he said softly.

She looked down at his hand, then at him. Hope. Yes, that's what this was. She couldn't feel like this and have it all be nothing. She had to know. She had to ask him. There was no point in playing coy games. Get it over with, she told herself. Just ask. But before she could form a question that would either destroy her or change her life forever, the car door was opened.

The driver was there, and Jack hesitated, then got out and she scooted across the seat and stepped out onto the sidewalk. At the same time she straightened, she heard and felt a throaty vibration in the air, a roar, and turned as four motorcycles came roaring down the street. They slowed, nosing into the curb one by one, in perfect formation, and then the engines died, and the men riding them got off.

Four men. All of them tattooed and wearing skull-caps, heavy boots, faded jeans with leather vests and shirts with cutoff sleeves. Trig, Jax, Bub, and Legs. Trig, the closest one, a mountain of man with wild gray hair escaping from the skull cap, spotted Rain, and the grin on his face said it all.

"Rainbow girl!" he boomed, coming toward her, and the next thing she knew, she was off her feet, in his arms, all but smothered in a bear hug.

The others were there, hugging and laughing, the scent of gasoline and fumes in the air. She could barely catch her breath, pleased to see all of them, but so uncomfortably aware of Jack behind her. She waited for the moment when she could explain that they were George's friends, that she'd known them since she was kid. But when she finally managed to turn while Trig was talking a blue streak, she didn't get a chance to explain anything to Jack.

He was at the entry to the warehouse, the door open. He hesitated, turned, looked right at her, then he went inside and closed the heavy metal door. She swallowed hard, and she felt whatever had been happening between them die an ugly death. Trig was hugging her again, saying something about George, asking about the possibility of bunking at the loft the way they always did when they were in town.

She nodded, barely hearing them as she tried to forget that last look from Jack. Wondering if what had just happened in the car had all been a dream.

JACK HEARD THEM next door well into the evening. Mary came and went, and Victoria was so tired she fell asleep watching TV. By ten, Jack was alone, and the party next door didn't show any signs of stopping. He couldn't begin to understand what he'd been doing tonight. The restaurant, the moment in the limo. It made no sense to him. He tried to work but he couldn't. By midnight, the sounds next door mellowed into slow music, and when he opened the windows, he heard voices on the fire escape landing.

Rain and various deep male voices. Probably the man she'd hugged downstairs. He had to force himself to move away from the windows, to a spot in the loft where he couldn't hear her voice. He sank down on the couch, sat forward and rested his head in his hands. When a loud thud sounded next door, followed by laughter, he reached for the phone on the side table.

He pushed away the images of holding Rain in the car, touching her and being engulfed by a need to make things right for her. It wasn't up to him to do anything. He put in the number, heard it ring four times, then Eve answered.

"Yes?"

"It's me."

"Oh, Jack," she said, no noise behind her this

time. "You just caught me on my way out. We're all going to Rags, a nightclub down here that's very…well…eclectic. What are you up to?"

"Can you talk for a bit?" he asked.

"They're ready to go, love."

He closed his eyes and heard himself saying, "I want you to come up here now," he said. He'd never begged for anything in his life, even when his father had dug a huge hole and Jack was struggling to get out of it. But he was close to begging at that moment. "Just for a day or two?"

"I'd love to," she said, "but they've got plans and this singer is coming down for a break. I don't know the singer, but they say he's fabulous and…" She lowered her voice. "Why don't you come down here for a break?"

"I can't."

Someone called something in the background, then there was a muffled response from her as her hand covered the phone. "Love? I need to go," she finally said into the phone. She hesitated, and he thought she was going to hang up, but she didn't. "Is something wrong?" she asked instead.

Wrong? He didn't know what to say. "I'd just like you to be here."

"Well, get your work done, then we can go on holiday together. The nanny can watch Victoria."

"I don't have a nanny. She didn't work out."

"Oh, no," she sighed. "What are you doing with the child while you work?"

It hit him that this was the first time she'd actually asked about Victoria, even though it wasn't directly about her well-being. "Taking care of her," he said.

''She's at the day care at LynTech. They have a therapist on staff at LynTech's day-care center, and she's been a huge help. Victoria's actually talking.''

''That's good,'' she said, but didn't sound too impressed. Someone yelled again, and she called back, ''Right there,'' then spoke into the phone. ''Have to scoot.''

''Sure,'' he said, and she was gone.

Jackson Ford was alone, and for the first time in his life, he really hated it.

Chapter Thirteen

"I'm really worried about Rain," Mary said as soon as Jack strode into the center the next day to pick up Victoria. The older lady, dressed all in blue, looked genuinely concerned. "She called and left a message on the machine that she wouldn't be in today. I thought it was because she didn't have a car and couldn't get here. Then I tried to call her back, but she didn't answer."

Jack had totally forgotten about her car being in the shop, but doubted that was why she hadn't come in. All he knew was when he and Victoria had left that the morning, the line of motorcycles was still there and no sounds came from the loft. "She's got company," he said.

Mary's face cleared a bit. "Oh, that could be it. Yes, that makes sense, if she has company."

He had no doubt that was the answer, as distasteful as it was to him. He looked at Victoria, the pink overalls he'd found in her suitcase, more appropriate than the dresses Eve had bought for her. She was drawing a picture of her doll, Emma. "Are you ready to go?" he asked.

This time she didn't pout. She just said in a little voice, "Can I stay?"

He looked at Mary, but saw that she was looking beyond him, and he turned to see Robert walking into the center. The dapper man in a dark charcoal three-piece suit, making his gray hair look even more startling in contrast, looked at Mary, but spoke to Jack as he approached them. "Didn't know you were here, Jack."

Jack had the distinct feeling Robert had hoped to find Mary alone. He didn't know why that shocked him. They were adults and they could do whatever they pleased, but he'd never known Robert to more than glance at a woman since his wife's death. "I came for Victoria," he said.

Ignoring Jack, Robert asked Mary, "Can you leave now?"

Color touched her cheeks. "No, I have things to do. I was just going to ask Jack if Victoria can stay with me while I work. We had a great time last night, and I kind of promised her that we would do some drawing today, maybe make paper dolls." She stopped the rush of words, looking at Jack and not at Robert. "Can she stay?"

Jack felt as if he was being used as a pawn, in a sense protecting her from Robert. But he found himself agreeing. "If she wants to."

"Thanks, Uncle Jack," Victoria said right away, then turned and plopped down on the floor, reaching for another piece of paper.

Mary smiled, a slightly tight expression. "Good, good, I'll bring her back later, and we'll get something to eat on the way home again." She glanced at

Robert. "You must have things to do, people to meet. I won't keep you."

Robert looked at Mary, then said evenly, "Have a nice evening." To Jack, he said, "I'll walk you out."

Jack thanked Mary, then went with Robert out of the center and the two stopped in the lobby. Jack thought Robert might have mentioned what was going on. But instead he said, "I guess things here are under control?"

Jack found the question ironic. Nothing seemed under control in his life. Then Robert said, "Sommers took his time, playing us for all we're worth, but finally came around."

Jack shrugged as they made their way to the glass entry doors to LynTech. "It looks that way, but we won't know for sure until he finalizes everything."

"He's coming in soon?"

Jack nodded. "Said he would. He's donating his Texas estate for the ball and will be attending, so he'll look over everything then."

Robert patted Jack on the shoulder. "You did it. You talked everyone into giving it another try."

"Everyone did it," Jack said. "But it wasn't easy."

Robert nodded. "A lesson learned, to tighten security when a deal is sensitive." He exhaled. "So, when are you heading home?"

Home? He knew he should feel relieved to be leaving Texas, but all he felt was tense. "I don't know," he murmured. "I think I need to stay to the end."

"You don't have to, Jack. It's all but a done deal. With any luck, it'll be finished by the ball."

"Luck? Since when did you depend on chance or

ever leave something unfinished when it could come back to hurt you later?''

Robert seemed to tighten at that question. ''You're right. I've only done that once, and—'' he shrugged ''—it always comes back. We'll just have to do what we can to minimize that possibility.'' He exhaled. ''Whatever happens, I think you need to get on with your life. You can't keep putting it on hold for LynTech. I've done that, and it doesn't work.''

Jack needed to get back on track, and get some stability in Victoria's life. ''I'll decide what I'm doing next week.''

''If I can do anything to help…''

He hesitated, then realized there was one thing Robert could help him with. ''There is something.'' He saw his car pull up to the curb. ''Do you need a ride?''

Robert glanced at the car, then back at Jack. ''Your car?''

''It's for my use.''

''Then I'll take the ride.''

''Good, I need to talk to you,'' Jack said and the two men headed out and went toward the parked car.

THE BIKERS STAYED at the loft over the weekend, and Rain didn't see Jack or Victoria during those two days. She heard them come and go, but other than that, she spent time with Trig and his buddies, picked up her car, talked about the old days. George called a couple of times to talk to the group, but he didn't offer to come back, or to meet them anywhere, which seemed a bit odd to Rain.

By late Sunday afternoon, Trig and the others were

packing to ride out early the next morning. When they took off to try to find a part for one of the bikes, Rain was finally alone. And she didn't like it at all. She found herself listening for sounds from next door, torn between wanting to connect with Victoria, to let the girl know that she was there, and having to be around Jack. She wandered around the loft, straightened up as best she could, and was just making herself some tea when there was knock at the door.

At first she thought she'd imagined it, but when it came again, she crossed to it. "Who's there?"

"Mary."

She pulled back the door and it was indeed Mary, and Victoria was with her. She'd been at Jack's. "What a nice surprise."

Mary smiled at her. "Victoria wanted to check and make sure you're okay before we left. She's been worried ever since you didn't show up at the center on Friday."

She crouched in front of the child, noticing that she was in jeans, a T-shirt and play shoes. A total change from the frilly dresses. "I'm just fine, sweetie. I've had company, so I couldn't be at the center." Even Emma had a new dress on. "You look lovely and so does Emma. Where are you off to?"

"A movie," Victoria said in her low voice. "I never been to one before."

"Well, they're magical, and you'll love it," she said.

"That's what I thought," Mary said with a smile.

Rain stood. "It's nice of you to take her."

"I have a new friend and she and her little girl need something to do, so I thought a movie would be nice. I think Mr. Ford needs some time to himself, so, I decided we'd all go.'' She put her hand on the child's shoulder. ''I'm surely going to miss her a lot when they go back to London next week.''

They were leaving. She knew they would. But she still felt an incredible sadness that this part of her life was over. Next week they'd go east and as she'd decided this weekend, she'd head to San Francisco. And that was that. ''We'll all miss her.''

''The show starts at five, then we're going to this pizza place that has games and things.'' She looked at her watch. ''We need to get going, but why don't you come with us?'' she asked.

She would love to spend more time with Victoria, but she couldn't. She needed to distance herself from the child, especially now that they'd be leaving soon. The way she had to with Jack. Just make space and not let anything else develop. ''Oh, thank you so much, but I can't. I've got company and they're not leaving until tomorrow. But, I'll be at the center tomorrow.'' She had to talk to Mary about leaving. That wouldn't be easy. ''You two have a good time and don't eat too much popcorn.''

The child smiled, a lovely, remarkable expression, given the permanent stamp of sadness she'd worn just a few days ago. Yes, not going to the movies was the right thing to do. It would be so easy to love this child, as easy as it was to love Jack. She couldn't afford to do either.

Victoria came closer, and when Rain crouched down again in front of her, the child hugged her tightly. It caught at Rain's heart. Oh, my, loving her wasn't just a possibility, it was a fact. Then Victoria stepped back, smiled at Rain, and said, "Bye-bye."

"Goodbye," she whispered, then watched Mary and Victoria cross to the elevator. The child waved as she got in and they started down. Rain waved, then turned and was about to reenter her loft, but stopped. She didn't hear anything, but she knew Jack was there. She could feel him, sense him, and when she turned, she was right.

There was no suit now, just dark slacks, a gray silk shirt, open at the neck and untucked, and bare feet. His hair was slightly spiked, as if he'd been running his fingers through it, and he stood there, more casual than she'd ever seen him, yet his dark eyes were so intense she had an impulse to run like mad. But she didn't.

The sight of him gave her pleasure that she couldn't define, and any ability to act rationally fled the moment he appeared. "I...I was talking to Victoria and Mary," she said.

He leaned against the doorjamb with his shoulder, one hand pushed into his pants pocket. He looked at the door to her loft. "Where's your company?"

"Out."

"Gone?"

"No, just out," she said, and knew she should explain about the arrival of Trig and company. She knew what he thought the instant he saw the wild bunch roaring up to the curb, and watched as Trig and the others hugged and kissed her. "You said before that we needed talk, and I think we do." It was he who hesitated this time, straightening, and almost stepping back. She knew he was going to refuse and suddenly she wanted him to understand things about her, before she left and this was totally over. "I need to tell you something."

She moved closer, regretting the action as soon as she inhaled his scent, as soon as she saw the fine lines fan at his eyes and bracket his mouth. He never stopped, never relaxed. And his effect on her never lessened.

"What did you need to tell me?" he asked.

She heard the door downstairs open and close with a heavy thud, then voices, but not anyone she knew. Probably the people in one of the lower units. Their laughter ran riot over her raw nerves, and she said, "Can we go inside and talk? Your place, my place? Just not out here?"

He nodded, then stood back and let her into his loft. She stepped past him, very careful not to touch him, then she heard the door close and she turned. He was less than two feet from her, both hands pushed into his pockets, rocking slightly on the balls of his feet. He was totally quiet, just waiting, and she suddenly didn't know what to say. "I need to explain some things to you," she finally said in a rush.

"You don't owe me any explanations," Jack murmured in a low voice. "What you do—and who you do it with—is your own business."

"Just what do you think I'm doing, and who do you think I'm doing it with? I thought we'd gone through this, you judging people, thinking you know what they are when you don't."

He shrugged. "I thought that's what you did."

They were arguing again, and she didn't know

why. She didn't want it to end like this. "Jack, I just
wanted to explain, and—"

"You don't have to."

"No, I don't have to," she said, her voice rising
just a bit. "But I want to, and I wish you'd do me
the favor of listening to me. I won't be here long. I'm
leaving for San Francisco the first of the week. I just
wanted to…to…" She wasn't sure what she wanted
to do or why she was even in here. What did it matter
what he thought of her? In a few days, he'd be on a
different continent.

"You're going back to California?" he asked,
coming closer.

"Yes, I am."

"You're giving up?"

"It's not a case of giving up, it's a case of I don't
have a job."

"When are you leaving?"

"Probably on Tuesday."

"You never know what can happen before then,"
he murmured. "What did you want to say?"

"About Trig and the others."

His expression tightened. "Forget it."

She looked right at him, and she knew exactly what
he'd been thinking. "You…you think that we…that
Trig and me, and the others…?" She swallowed hard.
"Oh, you're so wrong."

"Am I?" he breathed.

"Boy, are you ever. Trig is George's friend. They
met way back in the early seventies, and he's my
godfather, informally, but nonetheless, my godfather.
It was a ceremony in the woods up by the redwoods,
and he…" She waved a hand to cut off that rambling.
"The others, they're like uncles to me. They came to

see George about a gathering up north. They didn't even know I was here. And they're leaving tomorrow at dawn.''

He was closer, so close that she heard him take a breath before he spoke again. ''That's it? The biker gang is…what?''

''That biker gang is made up of an attorney, a sales rep, a package designer, and Trig, the head of his own corporation in Colorado. I never remember the name of it, but he got his nickname because he's a wizard at math and he's worth a lot of money.''

He shook his head. ''I'll be damned.''

''I surely hope not,'' she whispered, and looked right at him. In that moment she knew what she'd probably known all along…that she could love this man with all her heart. As it was, it was going to be misery walking away.

''Oh, Rain,'' he murmured. ''This is all…'' He shrugged sharply, then exhaled. ''I thought that you…that I was…''

She couldn't do this. Talking wasn't helping, and certainly, being so close to Jack wasn't, either. She had to leave before she did something that she she'd regret.

''You know, I should go. I have things to do, packing and stuff, and figuring out…'' Figuring out what her life was going to be from here on out.

Maybe Jack could read her expression, or maybe he had a way of looking into her soul, but he was shaking his head. ''No, no,'' he whispered, then came closer, cupping her chin gently in the heat of his hand. ''Don't go.''

She closed her eyes, trying to brace herself, trying

to block out the feeling of his touch. But she couldn't. Nor could she move. She couldn't do anything but stand there, connected in some way to this man that she didn't understand at all. She was startled when his lips touched hers, a tentative contact that was as light as a feather's caress, but as real as anything she'd ever felt.

"Stay," he breathed against her lips. "Please."

And she did. She let go of every reason to run, and of every shred of sanity that she possessed. That was the moment she knew that loving him wasn't an option. It was a fact. She loved him. She had fought it with every atom of her being and she was tired. She didn't have anything left in her to fight, and when she acknowledged that, she sagged toward Jack, into his chest, into his arms.

The minute he sensed her surrender, his lips traced along her cheek, finding a sensitive spot just under her ear, and he whispered roughly, "Thank you."

Rain trembled, and went to Jack, eyes wide-open. She knew what she was doing, and she didn't hesitate. This was for her, for all time, and she opened to him, tasted him, felt him and soaked his essence into her being. Her hands trailed over his back, down to his waist, then around to his stomach, tugging at his shirt, wanting to feel skin against skin. Heat against heat. Her heart against his heart.

Jack shifted and she was up in his arms, circling his neck, wrapping her legs around his hips, and he was carrying her, never stopping the kisses. Going back, and back, into shadows, together, and the next thing she knew they were on his bed, tangled in the linens, Jack over her. She felt as if he were a part of her. She reached up, tugging his shirt back and off his shoulders, reaching to kiss his naked chest, to taste his skin, relishing the heat, then feeling his heart against her lips.

He moved back, hesitating, then he was off the bed, standing over her, his shadowed eyes on her as he stripped off his shirt, then his slacks and stood there in his white briefs. He wanted her, that was obvious, but what she didn't understand was why. She knew why she wanted him, to have this time to take with her, to be hers after he was long gone to London, living his sane, elegant life with Eve.

That thought brought tears to her eyes and she reached for him, desperate for the contact again. He lay down beside her, and gathered her to him. With a gentleness that only intensified the tears, he slipped off her top, then eased down her jeans. Her bra clasp offered little resistance, and the lace was gone. His touch was on her naked skin, cupping her breasts, teasing her nipples. He eased his hands down, tucking them into the waistband of her panties.

She gasped as he pushed down the silk, looping his finger in the band, slipping it off her, tugging it away from the tangle at her feet. And she was naked. She lay very still, almost holding her breath as Jack eased higher and was looking down at her. His hands never stopped stroking, teasing, drawing feelings from her that she'd never experienced before. Never. She'd never lain like this with a man, never loved someone so much that she'd expose herself this way, down to her very soul.

The tears were silent, but didn't stop, and Jack leaned down, kissing them away, then taking the saltiness to her lips, invading her, possessing her. And his hand stroked her stomach, then moved lower and the moment he found her center, she gasped. She arched instinctively toward his touch, his palm pressing against her, slowly making circles that brought feelings that burned through her. Feelings that were all consuming, beyond anything she'd known in her life. His fingers entered her slowly, making her gasp, arch, tremble.

He moved over her. Then she felt his silky heat, wonderful pressure, and slowly, with aching care, he eased himself into her, and she couldn't breathe, she couldn't do anything but feel him, slowly filling her. The sensations bordered on pain, but went beyond, then suddenly he stopped. The world ground to a halt and she opened her eyes, looking up at him, his face not more than inches from hers, his eyes as dark as night.

"Please," she gasped, trying to pull him down to her, to hold him so tightly that she melted into him.

"Oh," he whispered. "You never…you…"

"Please," she said in a choked whisper. "Oh, Jack, please," she begged.

She wasn't sure what to do, how to do it, but instinctively she raised her hips to his. The movement brought a gasp from him, then a shudder and he buried his face in her tangled hair. He moved inside her, slowly, gently, until she wanted to cry out. The thrusts got faster, deeper and if the sensations before had been all encompassing, the ecstasy she found right then became the center of her world. The center of her soul.

She held on to Jack, lifting higher and higher, going into a place that both terrified and thrilled her. An unknown that she gladly followed Jack into. The next moment, as she climaxed, she understood that two human beings could become one, melded together in their souls. She cried out, held on to Jack, afraid to let go, then with one final thrust, she was his. Completely.

JACK LAY IN THE SHADOWS with Rain curled into his side, feeling more alive than he ever dreamed. This woman he'd been so wrong about was easing into his soul. He closed his eyes so tightly that colors exploded behind his lids. Wrong in so many ways.

Rain had never been with a man before. The image of the hippie commune and free sex wasn't what she was all about. She'd tried to tell him that, to let him know that she'd taken what she wanted from that culture, but lived life her own way. And he hadn't heard it. He hadn't understood. Maybe he couldn't have understood...not until now.

Now he understood what had been happening from the first moment he heard her voice. He'd been falling in love. Really falling in love, and fighting it at every turn. But in that one single, defining moment, it all made perfect sense. His whole life was altering, shifting and changing and he had no control over it. As she sighed softly, he knew that for the very first time in his life, he didn't want control. He wanted her in his life, a part of his life, to stay with him. Even if that meant living life her way. Any way she wanted them to live. But it had to be together. There had to be a chance of that.

He shifted slightly, pressed his lips to her forehead,

and tasted her. Then she stirred and he knew she wasn't asleep, either. He glanced at the clock. It would be a while before Mary brought Victoria home. Time enough. "What will your guests be thinking?" he murmured.

Rain shifted in his arms, twisting until she was pressed against him, her slender leg over his thighs, her hand resting against his heart and her hair tangling around them. "That I'm doing my own thing," she said on a soft chuckle. "When does Victoria come back?"

His breath caught when her hand moved lower. "Around eight and we…we have time…" He shuddered, every nerve ending in his body alive at her touch as her fingers splayed on his belly. "We need to talk."

"I know," she breathed, her touch finding his growing desire, and the contact brought him exquisite pleasure. "Oh, yes. But first," she breathed, shifting, kissing him over his heart. "First…" It wasn't talk that came next.

Rain was over him this time, her hair falling around them, as though enclosing them in their own world, and he lay there, letting her do what she wanted. What he craved. Touching him, kissing him. Doing things to him that brought shards of pleasure piercing his soul, catching his breath in his lungs.

There was an abandonment to her actions, almost a desperation, and he reached for her, the same feelings running through him. He had to have her, to know her again, to feel himself inside her, and she wanted the same thing. She shifted and he caught her by her waist, lifting her, easing her over him, then slowly lowering her onto him.

He filled her, and they both were still. He looked up at her, and knew with startling clarity that this was where he'd been headed all his life, toward this moment. With this woman. She moved, and he gasped, then together they moved, higher and higher, with a hunger that drove them both to the point of no return.

Then they were one, together, and nothing else mattered. Nothing.

Chapter Fourteen

Rain didn't want this feeling to stop. She didn't want to have to figure out what to do, what had happened, what could happen. She drifted in a delicious cocoon of sated desire, luxuriating in it, and in the feeling of Jack against her. She soaked up images and sensations, storing them away for a time when she couldn't reach out and touch him. When his heat was a memory, and the feeling of his weight over her, a blurred remembrance.

The sound of the buzzer for the entry door downstairs ripped through the loft, and it startled Rain. She sat up, Jack with her, in the darkness. "Mary and Victoria," he whispered, then he was touching her, giving her a quick, fierce kiss. "Get dressed."

He moved away from her, getting to his feet, and she watched him in the shadows, his nakedness taking her breath away. Then he was reaching for his slacks, dressing quickly. She followed suit. Jack reached out, brushed at her hair, and she could feel a certain unsteadiness in his touch.

The buzzer sounded again, and Jack cursed softly

under his breath. "Hurry," he said, and turned from her, jogging out to the other room.

She quickly raked her hair back with her fingers, twisted it into a knot, tucked it in to keep it in place, then finished dressing. By the time she stepped out into the living area, Jack was at the call box, hitting the button. "Yes?"

Nothing. He looked at her, then hit the button again. "Hello, is someone there?"

Nothing.

He exhaled in a rush, then turned to her, and watched as she crossed to him. "A prank," he muttered, then said softly, "You never cease to amaze me."

"How?" she asked, not daring to move any closer.

"I thought…" He shrugged, his words fading off. "You haven't been with anyone else, have you?"

That made her tremble slightly, but it was a truth that she had no trouble admitting. She'd never met anyone she wanted to be with until she met Jack. "That surprised you, didn't it?"

"Yes." A single word that hung between them, and made her tremble again.

A shiver shook her, and she hugged herself. "Of course it did," she muttered.

"Don't do that," he whispered roughly.

She looked at him, and her whole body ached. "What?"

"Think you know what I'm thinking, or going to say."

She bit her lip hard. "You weren't thinking that given my background and lifestyle, that I was sleeping with anyone who showed up? You sure thought that about Trig and his bunch.''

There was a banging on the door, and Jack jumped at the sound. He turned to grab the knob, but hesitated and said to Rain, ''We'll talk? Tonight, after Victoria's asleep, we can talk on the fire escape. Around ten?''

More knocking, but he didn't open the door.

''Okay?'' Jack persisted.

She finally said, ''Yes.''

The knocking came again, then a panicked voice called out, ''Jack, let me in. Let me in now! Jack!''

Rain saw the way he pulled at the handle, jerking the door open. That was when Rain finally saw Eve Ryder, in person.

Sickness clutched at her middle. Fantasy was one thing. But now reality had intruded, and she had to swallow hard to settle a violent lurch of nausea. Eve was just as beautiful as her pictures, tall and slender, wearing a dress that looked as if it cost a fortune. An ice-blue sundress that perfectly flattered her tanned skin and her long legs. In less than a heartbeat, Eve was in Jack's arms.

''Oh, thank God. I was so afraid you wouldn't be here.'' She even looked good on the verge of crying. ''Those…people. That huge man, and the motorcycles. He was right there with all those horrible tattoos, and he opened the door, and the taxi was leaving, and I…just hurried in. Then that elevator, and the cage, but I got in, and got the door down before he and the others were there.'' She shuddered, a delicate action. ''Goodness knows what they wanted or what they were going to do.'' She stood back slightly, her face flushed, etching her beauty more clearly. "Hurry, close that door," she said.

Jack swung the door shut and in doing so, let go of Eve completely. But he was still just inches from her, his body partially hiding Rain from Eve's view. "What are you talking about?"

"Oh, Jack," she said, exhaling. "That man, he just laughed and said something about his motorcycle, and the others…they were laughing when the elevator was going up." She shuddered again. "Good God, it was terrifying."

Jack rocked forward on the balls of his feet as he pushed both hands into his pockets. "You're okay, now," he said. "What are you doing here?"

"You asked me to come, silly."

"You said you couldn't." That tone she'd heard days earlier, when he'd been talking to Eve, was back. Not cold, but controlled, and not very pleased.

"Changed my mind," Eve said and Rain saw her flip her hand dismissively. "The party was off, because the singer never showed, so I thought it might be fun to run on up and spend a few days with you. I had no idea you were living in a place like this." The last part was said with real disdain as she looked around the loft. "What were they thinking of? Good grief."

That was when she saw Rain, and her whole expression shifted. She was shocked, but tried to hide it with a slight smile, an affected curve of her lips that didn't reach her eyes as she looked Rain up and down. Rain knew that she didn't miss her messy hair, or the way her shirt was untucked. But she didn't say a thing about it. Instead, she moved closer to Jack, pushing up against his side as she slipped her arm through his. "Oh, I'm sorry," she murmured with a touch of surprise, but total politeness in her voice. "I had no idea that you had company."

"This is Rain Armstrong, the therapist I told you was working at the center," Jack said, but he didn't look right at Rain. "She lives next door. Rain, this is Eve Ryder."

Eve held out a hand to Rain. "How lovely to meet you."

Before Rain could shake her hand, someone pounded on Jack's door, a cracking, booming sound. Eve turned, her eyes wide. "Oh, God, they followed me!" she said, and Rain thought Eve might actually dive behind Jack for protection.

"Who's there?" Jack called out.

"Trig."

Rain moved around both of them, and opened the door. "Rainbow," he said. "A lady downstairs ran up here and I wanted to let her know that..." He smiled past Rain. "There you are. Sorry to scare you, ma'am," he said politely. "I was just letting her in, trying to help."

"Yes, of course," Eve said, gaining a bit of control when she saw that Rain and Jack weren't calling the police. She looked at Jack. "Rainbow?"

Rain turned. "Rainbow Swan Armstrong, and this is Trig, my godfather."

"Oh," Eve said, elongating the single word softly.

Rain didn't look at Jack. She couldn't. The moment was gone, over. She looked at Trig, but spoke to the other two. "I'll be going," she said, then left the loft.

The door swung shut after her, but not before she

heard Eve say, ''Good grief, and you let her be around Victoria?''

She never heard Jack's reply, which was probably just as well. Reality hit her hard. Eve and Jack fit. He was engaged to Eve. He was going to marry her. She'd known that all along. She'd just hidden from it, temporarily, when they'd made love.

Trig was in her loft, and she was in the hallway, almost unable to move. She couldn't go inside and joke and visit with Trig and the others, not when she was having to hug her arms around her middle to try not to think about what had just happened. As though on cue, the door to Jack's loft suddenly opened. Rain turned and he was there.

He came toward her, stopping within inches. ''I didn't know about this, about Eve coming,'' he said in a low, rough whisper.

She ached with the need to touch him again, but she didn't act on it. Her fingers dug into her upper arms. ''Let's pretend this never happened, and you go back to Eve.''

He closed his eyes, then took a breath and looked at her. ''That's ridiculous,'' he muttered. ''We'll talk. Ten, on the fire escape.''

She was going to cry and desperately wanted to escape. ''No,'' she barely whispered. ''No.''

''Rain, you need—''

''No,'' she snapped. ''Don't you dare try to tell me what I need. I'm not something you have to fix!''

A muffled buzzer sounded, then the door to his loft opened. Eve looked out, and said, ''Jack, did you—'' She saw Rain and her words stopped abruptly. ''Did you find it?''

He shook his head without turning to Eve. "No, I didn't. I must have left it in the car."

"Oh, well. A lady just buzzed. She and Victoria are on their way up."

Rain heard the elevator groan on its way to pick up Mary and Victoria. She didn't want to see either of them, and she turned without saying a word. Jack didn't say anything else, and when she closed the door, safe in George's loft, she was thankful for the heavy barrier. But even that couldn't keep out the muffled sounds of Mary and Victoria arriving, and she shuddered.

Her whole life was in pieces and she'd done it to herself. She couldn't justify any of her actions, except pleading insanity. She hugged herself again and turned. Trig was there, ten feet away, watching her. The others were sitting on the floor, packing what looked like pieces of a motor into boxes. "Who's that guy and that...hysterical woman?" Trig asked.

"It's a long story," she murmured, the faint touch of engine oil mixing with the other odors in the loft, testing her stomach again.

"I've got time," he said.

She shook her head. "No, it's okay. I'm okay." The lie tightened in her throat. "Did you get all your parts?"

"Sure did. Legs has got it all under control."

"Good. Good," she said, and wished she was alone. Then, as if Trig had heard her thoughts, she was about to get her wish.

"If you're okay, we were thinking of pushing on up north tonight as soon as we can roll up the beds. We got a connection with a guy up there who's doing work on a classic bike and he needs some help. We'll meet up with your dad next time.''

''George will be sorry he missed you.''

He reached in his pocket and handed her the key she'd given him earlier. ''Good thing I had that. The lady was ready to have a breakdown,'' he said, with a bit of a smug smile that sort of confirmed something Rain had always thought about Trig. He got some perverse pleasure having people cringe just a bit when he came close. No one would ever guess how gentle he really was, or how corporate he could be in business. All they saw was his image.

They left half an hour later, and Rain stood alone at the curb as they roared off. She turned, ready to go back inside, then stopped. She had her bag with her, and her keys. Instead of heading upstairs, she got into her car and drove off.

She ended up sitting through a movie that she couldn't remember the moment she left, then getting something to eat at Our Place. Afterward she stayed for a long time and talked with Lizard. She listened to all the stories she'd heard many times before, but she didn't care. It helped not to have to think.

By the time she got back to the loft, it was after midnight, and she was well aware that she'd missed her talk with Jack. She checked the phone. Four calls, all from an unknown caller, but no messages. She turned and heard Joey was meowing at the windows. She let him in, fed him and he stayed, which surprised her. He usually bummed food then ran. When she finally curled up to sleep in the hammock, the cat lay down with her, purring uproariously. She left the small television on to cover any noise from next door and eventually drifted off to sleep.

When she opened her eyes again, someone was knocking on the corridor door. She pushed herself up and sat there, listening but not moving. Then she heard Jack call, "Rain, are you in there?" and she ignored it. She closed her eyes tightly, held her breath, and barely breathed again until he stopped talking, stopped knocking and she heard the elevator going down.

She didn't move until Joey squalled and she saw him at the window wanting to go out. She looked at the clock. Almost ten. Jack usually left so much earlier, but then again, he'd never had Eve there in the morning before. She scrambled out of the hammock, let the beast out, then showered and got dressed in jeans and a yellow pullover she wore with her boots. Her throat ached and her eyes burned and she felt as if she had a hangover, but she was going to the center. She had to say goodbye.

As she crossed to the door to leave, the phone rang. She checked the caller I.D. and saw it was the Children's Hospital. When she answered it, Dr. Shay's secretary was on the other end. Quickly, she told her that Dr. Shay needed her to come by his office as soon as possible. The woman didn't say why, and Rain didn't ask. It was the official brushoff, she knew that, cementing the fact that they couldn't hire her on staff.

She agreed to stop by in half an hour, then hung up and left. When she got to the Children's Hospital, it was alive with activity, with the rhythm unique to a hospital, and she realized how very much she missed her hospital work. She'd loved the time with Victoria and Mary and the other kids, but this is what she wanted to do. She could hire on in the Bay area when she got back to the Coast. With that thought she found herself at Dr. Shay's office in the business administration wing, and his secretary told her to go right in.

She stepped into the doctor's private office and he rose from behind a painfully modern glass desk. A thin, gray-haired man, with a pinched face and pale skin, Dr. Shay nodded to her. "Thank you for coming on such short notice," he said without a smile.

The other times she'd been here, she'd been struck by the man's coolness. Hardly a good bedside manner, she'd thought more than once, but knew that a doctor could have the personality of a turnip as long as he was good at what he did. "I wanted to talk to you anyway," she said.

He motioned her to one of the chairs that faced the desk. "Please, sit."

He began right away. "I'll just get to the point. I am very happy to tell you that funding for your appointment has been approved. Welcome to our staff." She was certain her shock must have been more than evident, but he didn't react at all. "If you can come in tomorrow morning, we'll bring you up to speed."

She heard his words, but couldn't for the life of her figure out how to react. She had what she'd been waiting for, but suddenly she wasn't sure she was going to take it or why it materialized just like that, almost out of thin air. "You have funding? I thought you…I mean, you said…"

"I am so sorry for the delay and any inconvenience

it caused you. I, myself, never thought we could pull this off, but we desperately need someone of your caliber working here.''

''How did you pull it off?'' she asked with more bluntness than she intended.

His expression tightened slightly. ''Well, let's just say that you have some very influential friends who really believe in what you can do for us.''

That made no sense. ''Excuse me?''

''Mr. Lewis from LynTech has been so wonderful to us. His donations, using his influence on our behalf, and then the upcoming charity ball...'' He actually smiled at the mention of Robert Lewis's kindnesses to the hospital. ''The man is incredible.''

''What does Mr. Lewis have to do with my position here?''

''Well, I guess it's no secret and he certainly didn't ask me to keep it quiet. The fact is, he's adding funding to make sure you can get on board. He was adamant about it.''

Robert Lewis? She'd barely talked to the man. He didn't know her beyond the few words they'd exchanged at the center. Dr. Shay stood, extending his hand to Rain. ''May I welcome you to the staff?''

She stood and took his hand, but found herself stammering somewhat. ''I...I think so, but I'll need to see about some things. Can I get back to you this afternoon?''

He looked as perplexed as she felt when she didn't jump at the offer. But he simply nodded. ''Of course.''

She left, trying to figure out what was going on as she made her way to LynTech. By the time she got there, she still had more questions than answers. She went in through the main reception area, and stopped by the guard's station, to ask if Mr. Lewis was in. The man nodded, said that Robert Lewis had come in about an hour ago, and that he'd gone upstairs, probably to the top floor.

Rain hurried over to the elevators, and headed upstairs. She knew there was a chance Jack might be there, too, but didn't hesitate. She needed answers.

Rain hurried down the hall to Matthew Terrell's office. If anyone knew where Mr. Lewis was, it would be Rita. But the office reception area was empty, and the open door to the private office showed it was empty, too.

She went back into the hallway and headed down toward Mr. Holden's office. When she went in there, she found Rita at the desk. She looked up and smiled at Rain. "Well, hello. If you're looking for Victoria, she's not here."

She shook her head. "I was actually trying to find Mr. Lewis."

"Well, I just got here, but the last I heard, they were all in the conference room with Mr. Sommers. He just got in and things are crazy. This is the first chance I've had to sit and get things in order."

That meant Jack was in the meeting, too. Ignoring that thought, Rain knew she couldn't wait for Mr. Lewis to come out. He could be in there for hours. "Well, thanks, I'll try to catch him later."

Rita reached for the phone and said, "I can ring in to ask him to come see you."

"Oh, no, please, don't do that. I don't want to interrupt him."

Rita hesitated, then put the phone back on the hook and reached for a pink pad laying by the phone. ''Well, wait a moment,'' she said, pulling the pad closer to her. ''It's a note from Mr. Lewis. He says that if a call comes in for him, to route it down to the day-care center.'' She looked at Rain. ''That's odd. I was sure he'd be in the meeting.'' She shrugged. ''But he's apparently downstairs.'' Rita got up. ''I need to get down to legal, but you're welcome to use the phone to call down there for him.''

''Thanks,'' Rain said and moved to pick up the phone as Rita came around the desk.

Rita motioned into the private office. ''When you leave to go down, why don't you take the private elevator? It's direct and you'll come out right by the back entrance to the center. I use it all the time.''

''Thanks,'' she said. Rita left and Rain dialed the center. Mary answered after several rings. ''Rain, I was getting worried when you didn't come in on time.''

''Oh, I'm sorry, but I overslept, then I had to go to the hospital.''

''Are you at the hospital now?''

''No, I'm upstairs. I was looking for Mr. Lewis.''

''He just left. He was talking to Mr. Ford, then he and Anthony left together, something about a train tunnel.''

Jack was down at the center? That didn't make sense, either. ''I'll catch up with him later,'' she said and would have hung up, but Mary caught her before she could say goodbye.

''Are you coming down to the center now?''

Not with Jack there. "No, I don't think so. It sounds as if you've got enough people down there."

"Not really. Mr. Lewis left and Mr. Ford left with Miss Ryder, something about the airport. My goodness, she's a beautiful woman. I forgot he was engaged. And Victoria...well, she didn't seem to know how to act with the woman, but I guess that will change once they're married."

Rain felt her legs go weak and it was all she could do to get to the chair Rita had vacated, and sink down into it. "The airport?"

"Miss Ryder was saying that the flight was leaving soon."

Rain closed her eyes so tightly they ached, but it was better than tears of weakness escaping again. She was tired of crying, and tired of feeling so damn empty and alone. He was gone. It was over. Just like that. It didn't matter if she took the job here or went back to California. It just didn't matter. And she never got to say goodbye to Victoria. Her eyes stung and it took her a moment to realize that Mary was still talking to her.

"Rain, are you—"

"I...I'll come by tomorrow morning, and we'll talk." She hung up quickly, but couldn't stand for a while. When she finally felt her legs would support her, she stood, intending to leave and call Robert Lewis later on. But another note caught her eye. It was a folded piece of paper with Jack's name on the front, and a glimpse of her name where the paper parted.

She picked it up, sinking back in the chair and read, "Jack, I contacted Dr. Shay and Dr. Armstrong will be hired on today. It's all settled. Glad to help. Robert.'' She stared at it, each word dark and imprinted in her mind. Jack had put Robert Lewis up to getting her hired. She was shaking and tossed the note back on the desk so she could clasp her hands tightly in front of her. Jack had negotiated the job for her. A favor? Had it cost him money? Her stomach lurched. Was it payment for…? She couldn't finish the thought. It was too ugly. She took several deep breaths, waited, then pushed herself to her feet and headed for the private elevator. She knew what she had to do.

Rain didn't get back to the loft until well after nine that evening. Her meeting at the hospital was prolonged and not pleasant, then she went by the restaurant to say goodbye to Lizard and ended up telling him everything…almost. She told him about Jack, but not about sleeping with him. She told him about Jack leveraging Lewis to get her hired on. And she told him she'd just refused the job and was leaving for California the next day. He listened, shook his head, then told her what she knew. ''You don't need what you found here, Rainbow. Maybe the Coast is the best place for you now.'' He'd been right. She didn't need any of what she'd found in Houston. Nothing here was hers.

Chapter Fifteen

When Rain finally got back to the loft, she changed into her sleeping shirt then set about packing, knowing she was doing the right thing, but feeling as if she were giving up. She hated that. She wasn't a quitter, but then again, there wasn't anything here to fix. Besides, Jack was the fixer. The one who thought she needed saving. Or to be paid off. Either way, she didn't need it or want it.

The phone rang four times after she got home, all calls from an unknown caller, and she chose not to answer it. Jack was on his way to England, and she really didn't want to talk to anyone right now. When it stopped ringing the last time, she glanced at the clock and it was midnight. She needed air and crossed to the fire escape door. When she stepped out onto the cold metal, she heard the cat. She turned and saw Joey over on Jack's landing, batting at the closed window and squalling loudly. She looked at the higher windows and they were all shut, so he was closed out completely.

"Hey, Joey," she said, and he turned and looked at her. "Come on over here." She actually wanted the company. "I'll feed you," she said, bribing the orange cat.

He turned back to the window, batted it with his paw and meowed again. He looked at her, then did it again.

"There's no one there," she said. "Come on over here."

He hit the window again, meowing plaintively.

She exhaled. "Okay, okay, I'll be right over," she said and went inside. She found the key to the other loft, but after she unlocked it she almost couldn't go inside. Her legs felt weak, and there was a tightness in her chest. Then she forced herself to go forward into the shadows, and the minute she was inside, she could feel Jack.

It was crazy, as if the essence of the man lingered there in the air like some ghost intent on torturing her. She stopped, took a breath, then leaving the door partially open, she crossed the cool wooden floor as quickly as she could. She didn't look left or right in the shadows, but straight ahead toward the windows.

When she reached the fire escape window, she opened it and the cat dived inside. He sailed past her, hitting the only clear space on the worktable with one graceful leap and without making a sound. He stopped, looked at her, then jumped to the floor and disappeared into the kitchen.

"Great," she muttered. "A manipulative cat," and realized that she had to contact Zane Holden to let him know that no one would be here to care for Joey after tomorrow. Then again, maybe the man would agree to let her adopt the beast and take him back to California with her. He was a survivor and she liked that about him, no matter how annoying he could be at times.

She went after the cat, glancing to her left without thinking and seeing the screen that had been used to hide Victoria's bed. Her throat clenched and she made herself go into the kitchen. It had been so wrong of Jack, no matter what had gone on with them, to leave without letting her say goodbye to Victoria. It just wasn't fair. Then again, life wasn't fair. It never had been.

She crossed to the counter, and in the moonlight, she opened some food for Joey and placed it on the floor.

"Enjoy it," she said softly. "But listen, we have to have a talk. You can't be here any longer, and neither can I, and despite the fact that you drive me crazy, I was thinking of talking to Mr. Holden to see if he'd let you come with me to California. Would you like to go to the Coast? I hear the grade of mice there is pretty darn good." He never stopped eating and she sighed. "Well, I've lost it, standing here in the dark talking to a cat."

"I thought I heard your voice."

For a moment, she really thought she'd lost it, that she'd dragged a ghost into the room. But when she turned, Jack was in the doorway surrounded by shadows. Almost unreal. But the moment was achingly familiar. She in here, feeding the cat, he sneaking up on her, half-dressed. He came closer, and she knew how very real he was in his pajama bottoms, watching her, so close that all she had to do was reach out. She clenched her hands into tight fists. "I...I thought you were gone," she said.

"Shhh," he moved closer again, so close that he could put his forefinger softly on her lips. "Victoria's sleeping. She's very upset that she didn't see you today, and she went over to your place when we got home, but you weren't there. She had me call over and over again, but you didn't answer."

She moved, trying to break the contact. He drew back easily, and exhaled roughly. "You weren't there this morning, either. Or at ten o'clock last night on the fire escape. And now you're in here feeding the beast."

She could barely breathe, and was overwhelmingly thankful that he'd only touched her for a brief moment. "Mary…she said you were going to the airport, and I thought… I heard Joey and he was hungry and he wouldn't come in to my place, and then…" She shrugged. "Why aren't you in London?"

"Because I'm here, and I think I'm staying in the area. That's to be worked out." He held his hand out to her and she looked down and saw her anklet looped over his forefinger. "You forgot this."

She reached for it, jerking it free, but in the process breaking it at the clasp. "Oh, shoot," she muttered. "You broke it."

"You broke it."

She looked up at him, closing her hand over the woven yarn. She'd thought she'd lost it somewhere, but never thought that she'd lost it in his bed. "I broke it," she said on a sigh.

"What now?"

"I guess George can get it fixed, or maybe—"

"No, I wasn't asking about the anklet."

"Oh, I'm leaving. I'll leave you alone."

He shook his head, but didn't move to let her go. "There you go again, thinking you know what I'm saying, what I'm thinking, and being dead wrong…again."

She exhaled. "It doesn't matter. I thought you and Eve were…" She bit her lip. "You went to the airport, didn't you?"

"I took Eve there for her flight out to Acapulco. She's got parties to attend and people to meet and fun to have."

Her stomach knotted and she hugged her arms around her middle. "What about you?"

"Me? I've got things to do here, important things." His voice dropped lower and he was so close she could have sworn that she could see a pulse beating at the base of his throat.

"Oh, of course," she whispered. "I know what you've been doing. Pressuring Mr. Lewis to bribe Dr. Shay into hiring me on." She was clutching her upper arms so tightly that her fingers were digging into her flesh. "You shouldn't have bothered. I turned it down."

"You what?"

"Refused it," she snarled through clenched teeth. "I won't take a payoff from you. I didn't want you to make things right for me, to bribe the man with funds for the wing at the hospital. I told you before, I didn't need you to fix my life, to rescue me or save me from myself."

He was so still, so quiet that she started to tremble. That was when he reached out, touching her on the shoulders, and she jerked back. "Oh, no," she gasped.

He didn't try to touch her again, but he didn't move back, either. "Okay, you're right," he whispered in such a low voice that she could barely make out what he was saying. "You don't need fixing, you don't need rescuing or saving. You never have." He took an unsteady breath. "But I do."

"What...what are you talking about?"

"What I am, what I was becoming."

"Jack, I don't—"

"Just listen to me, please," he said.

"Jack, I'm leaving for California tomorrow, and I need to get back to—"

He touched her again, his forefinger on her lips, and she felt her breath catch in her chest. "Please," he breathed.

She closed her eyes, then nodded and the connection was gone. When she opened her eyes, he'd moved away a bit, back into the partial shadows, facing her. Then he ran both hands roughly over his face, and said in a low voice, "I don't know how to do this. But I can't let you leave without making sure that you understand things."

"What things?" she asked, not sure what he was trying to say.

He came closer again, and framed her face with both his hands. She didn't dare move because all she could think of was taking one step toward him and letting herself sink into his arms. "You...me... important things."

She closed her eyes tightly. "Oh, Jack, no..."

His thumbs moved on her skin, soft and gentle. "Oh, yes. Listen to me. I heard your voice in here, the way I heard you that first night, and I have to tell you something. I think from the moment I heard you whispering to that cat, you seduced me.''

She kept her eyes scrunched tightly shut.

''Rainbow Swan, I need you. Rescue me?'' he whispered in an unsteady voice. ''Please?'' She felt his breath brush her face, then his lips touched hers, a mere suggestion of a kiss, and it was gone.

She opened her eyes and he was there, watching her intently and she felt the vague unsteadiness in his hands. No, it didn't matter that her heart literally hurt at that moment. It didn't matter at all. This was crazy, and she wasn't going to let anything happen again. She wasn't sure she'd survive if she had to walk away from him one more time.

She moved back as best she could, and his hands let her go, but he didn't move away. ''I...I'm going and I really wish that you'll have a terrific life, and that Victoria will be happy and...'' Her voice broke and she felt the tears on her cheeks, but she didn't make a move to wipe them away. ''Please, I just have to go.''

He exhaled. ''No.''

The single word hung between them and she felt the counter pressing into her waist. She didn't have a choice. ''Whatever.''

''God, I hate that word,'' he muttered, then she could see him trying to calm down. Finally, he said, ''Rain, I was getting married and I thought it was the right thing to do...until you. Until you showed up right here, in the middle of the night and showed me what life was all about. I've been so sure of everything, so confident that I knew what I wanted, then you changed all of that. From the first, you worked your way into my life…and into my heart." He laughed roughly. "God, I'm not a poetic man, but I'm actually waxing profound at the moment. This is crazy."

"Eve?" She could only manage the one word.

"She's gone. We had a long talk and she was actually very good about it when I told her. She spent the night at a hotel and at the airport she said something about fearing for my life if I got involved with someone who had a motorcycle gang to back her up."

She couldn't laugh. "She's gone?"

"Back to her parties and her friends. I told her that I wasn't in love with her. That I didn't know what being in love meant until I met you." He exhaled. "God, I never knew what this was. Never. Not until you."

He loved her? "What?" she breathed.

"You, with your meditation, and your biker gang, and your hippie father and your horrible tea." He leaned down and kissed her quickly, but before she could catch his taste on her tongue, the contact was gone, but he never let go of her. His hands on her were unsteady as he breathed, "I want you, Rainbow Swan. I want you in my life forever, and in Victoria's. But we absolutely have to live in the same city. That's not negotiable. I couldn't do what George does, having semiannual visits, and knowing you were someplace else. I have to insist on the same city at least."

"Oh, my," she breathed, and as his words sank in and became real, her legs gave out. The next thing she knew she was in Jack's arms, and he was lifting her high off the ground. She wrapped her legs around his hips, and buried her face in his chest. "Oh, my," she said again, with feeling. "Oh, my."

JACK HELD HER TO HIM, relishing the feel of her in his arms, loving her so completely that it stunned him. The last twenty-four hours had been horrible, first explaining things to Eve, then trying so hard to find Rain and make her listen to him. "Would you give me a chance?" he asked, his voice muffled in her hair. "It's not easy for me, being spontaneous and throwing caution to the wind. But damn it, I'm willing to try, if you'll have me?"

She shifted, titling her head back to look into his eyes. "Do you love me?" she asked in a husky voice. "Really love me?"

"That's what I've been trying to tell you," he said.

"But do you love me?" she asked in a low whisper. "Can you tell me you love me?"

He looked at her, and knew saying these words was the easiest thing he'd ever done in his life. "I love you." Then he said, "Your turn," and he felt his breath catch in his chest.

"Oh, I love you, Jackson whatever-your-middle-name-is Ford."

"Penn, my middle name is Penn, my mother's maiden name."

"Jackson Penn Ford," she murmured, then her lips found his and the only sound in the loft was Joey starting to meow again.

"Joey's crying."

Jack jerked back from the kiss, and Rain scrambled out of his hold to stand on the floor as he turned to see Victoria in the doorway in her nightgown, holding the doll. "You're awake?" he said.

"I heard you." She looked at Rain and her bottom lip protruded in a definite pout. "You were gone."

"I'm here now," Rain said, crossing to the child and crouching down in front of her. "I'd never go anywhere without telling you first."

Victoria stared at her, then looked at Jack. "Uncle Jack?"

He went closer, and he had to touch Rain, just to confirm that she was real and she was here. He crouched by her and put an arm around her. Her hand came up to cover his where it rested on her upper arm. "What, Victoria?"

"Can Rain stay?"

"Stay?"

"Here, with you and me?"

Jack looked at Rain, so close, and said, "That's up to Rain."

Rain looked from him to Victoria, then back at him again. Her hand over his tightened perceptibly. "If you both want me to, I'd love to. Are you sure that's what you want, Victoria?"

She looked at Jack, then moved closer to Rain. "Oh, yes, please," she said softly.

"Save us both, Rain?" Jack whispered.

He saw her swallow, then said, "Only if you'll rescue me right back."

He laughed with relief, reaching out to hug Victoria and the doll to him and Rain, enfolding them both in his arms. "Well, that sounds like a plan," he said. "Doesn't it, Victoria?"

The cat was there, pressing between them and Victoria bent down to pat him. ''Joey, too?'' she asked.

''Joey, too,'' Jack said.

Victoria looked up at both of them. ''We'll all get married?''

Jack felt Rain tense, then she leaned into him and said, ''That sounds good to me, but it's up to Uncle Jack.''

''You mean it?'' he breathed.

She tilted her head up, looking right at him. ''With all my heart.''

He exhaled a breath he hadn't realized he'd been holding, and said, ''Then, yes, we'll all get married.'' And for the first time ever, Jack's life made perfect sense.

* * * * *

Look for the next book in Mary Anne Wilson's
JUST FOR KIDS *miniseries,*
WINNING SARA'S HEART,
in February 2004.

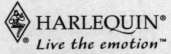

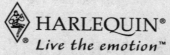

National Bestselling Author

brenda novak

COLD
FEET

Despite the cloud of suspicion that followed her father to his
grave, Madison Lieberman maintained his innocence...*until* crime
writer Caleb Trovato forces her to confront the past once again.

**"Readers will quickly be drawn into this well-written,
multi-faceted story that is an engrossing, compelling read."**
—*Library Journal*

Available February 2004.

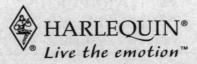

HARLEQUIN®
Live the emotion™

Visit us at www.eHarlequin.com

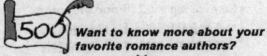

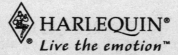

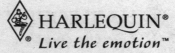